TWICE AS MUCH AS MET
THE EYE LAST TIME!

CHEE CHOO

INCREDIBLE CHANGE!
CHOO
CHEE
CHOOK
BEW.

 PUBLISHED BY TOP SHELF PRODUCTIONS, P.O. BOX 1282, MARIETTA, GA 30061-1282, USA. PUBLISHERS: BRETT WARNOCK AND CHRIS STAROS. VISIT OUR ONLINE CATALOG AT WWW.TOPSHELFCOMIX.COM

ISBN 978-1-60309-067-4
1ST PRINTING. MARCH 2011.
PRINTED IN SINGAPORE.

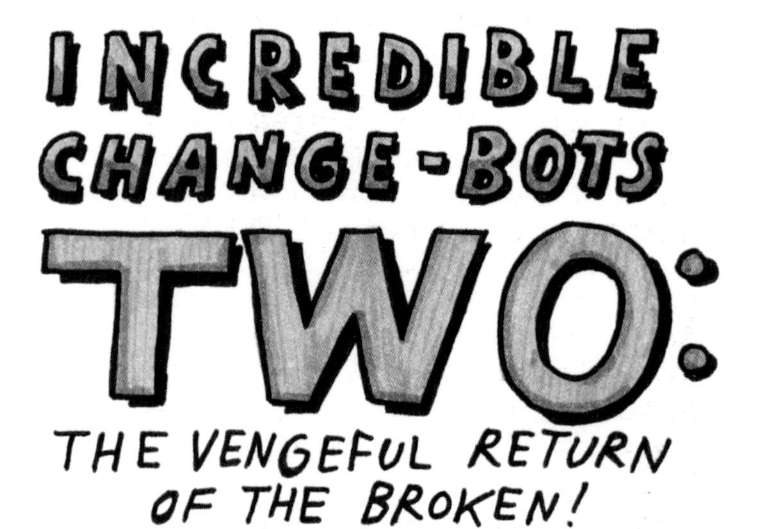
INCREDIBLE
CHANGE-BOTS
TWO:
THE VENGEFUL RETURN
OF THE BROKEN!

FAR AWAY FROM EARTH BUT NOT TOO LONG AGO*, THERE WAS A PLANET KNOWN TO ITS INHABITANTS AS: ELECTRONOCYBERCIRCUITRON!
* DEPENDING ON WHEN YOU READ THIS

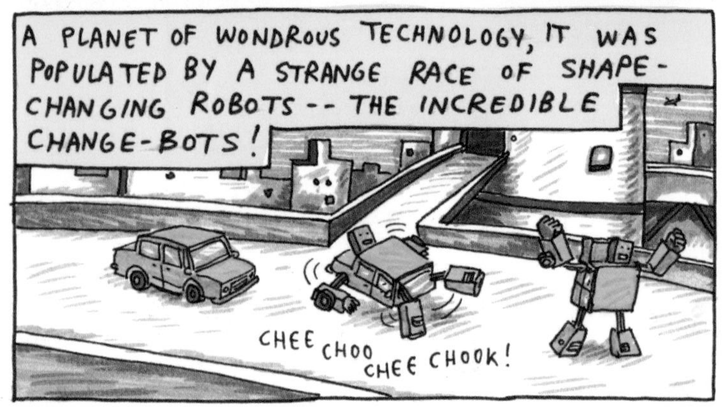
A PLANET OF WONDROUS TECHNOLOGY, IT WAS POPULATED BY A STRANGE RACE OF SHAPE-CHANGING ROBOTS -- THE INCREDIBLE CHANGE-BOTS!
CHEE CHOO CHEE CHOOK!

THERE WERE TWO GROUPS OF CHANGE-BOTS. FIRST, THE AWESOMEBOTS, WHO PRIDED THEMSELVES ON THEIR LEADERSHIP AND TRIED TO MAKE ELECTRONOCYBERCIRCUITRON THE GREATEST WORLD ON THE PLANET!

SECOND WERE THE FANTASTICONS, WHO WERE POWER-HUNGRY AND WISHED TO TAKE CONTROL FROM THE AWESOMEBOTS, IN ORDER TO MAKE THEIR BELOVED ELECTRONOCYBERCIRCUITRON THE GREATEST PLANET THAT EVER LIVED!

UNABLE TO AGREE ON SEVERAL INSIGNIFICANT DETAILS, THE AWESOMEBOTS AND FANTASTICONS WAGED A FIERCE WAR AGAINST EACH OTHER!
BDEW!
BEW!
BEW!
BEW!
RAZOW!
WITH THEIR PLANET DECIMATED, THE CHANGE-BOTS SET ASIDE THEIR DIFFERENCES AND LEFT TO LOOK FOR A NEW HOME...
WE COULD CLEAN ALL THIS UP...
NAH, IT'D BE EASIER TO JUST START FRESH.

...BUT INSTEAD CRASHED ON PLANET EARTH, WHERE THEIR BICKERING BEGAN AGAIN.
OUCH
WHILE THE AWESOMEBOTS MADE NEW FRIENDS,
BEEP BEEP!
THE FANTASTICONS MADE NEW ALLIES.
WE'D LOVE TO WORK WITH YOU.
THE CHANGE-BOTS HAD BROUGHT THEIR DEVASTATING WAR TO EARTH!
BEW!
BEW!
BEW!
BEW!
BEW!
BEW!
BDEW!
BEW!
BEW!
BEW!
BEW!
BEW!
BEW!
BDEW!
BEW!

THE TWO WARRING SIDES FINALLY MET IN A CLIMACTIC FINAL BATTLE FINALE!
BEW!
BEW!
BEW!
BEW!
SHOOTERTRON, LEADER OF THE FANTASTICONS, WAS DEFEATED...
AIEEEEEEEEEE!
BIG RIG AND THE AWESOME-BOTS WERE VICTORIOUS!
WE'RE AWESOMEBOTS TOO
YEAH, WE WERE, LIKE, SPIES.
THE CHANGE-BOTS ONCE AGAIN SET OUT TO SEARCH FOR A NEW HOME.
sniff

LATER...
ERGH
WHERE AM I? WHA-- WHAT HAPPENED?
HOW DID I GET HERE? AND... WHO AM I?
AND EVEN MORE IMPORTANTLY...
WHY DO I EXIST?

THE DAZED SHOOTERTRON STUMBLES FORWARD, CONFUSED AND UNCERTAIN...
IS THIS WHAT I SHOULD DO? SHOULD I HAVE STAYED WHERE I WAS?
WHAT AM I DOING? WHERE AM I GOING?
WHAT PURPOSE IS THERE TO ANY OF THIS?
I DON'T... FEEL... SO... GOOD...

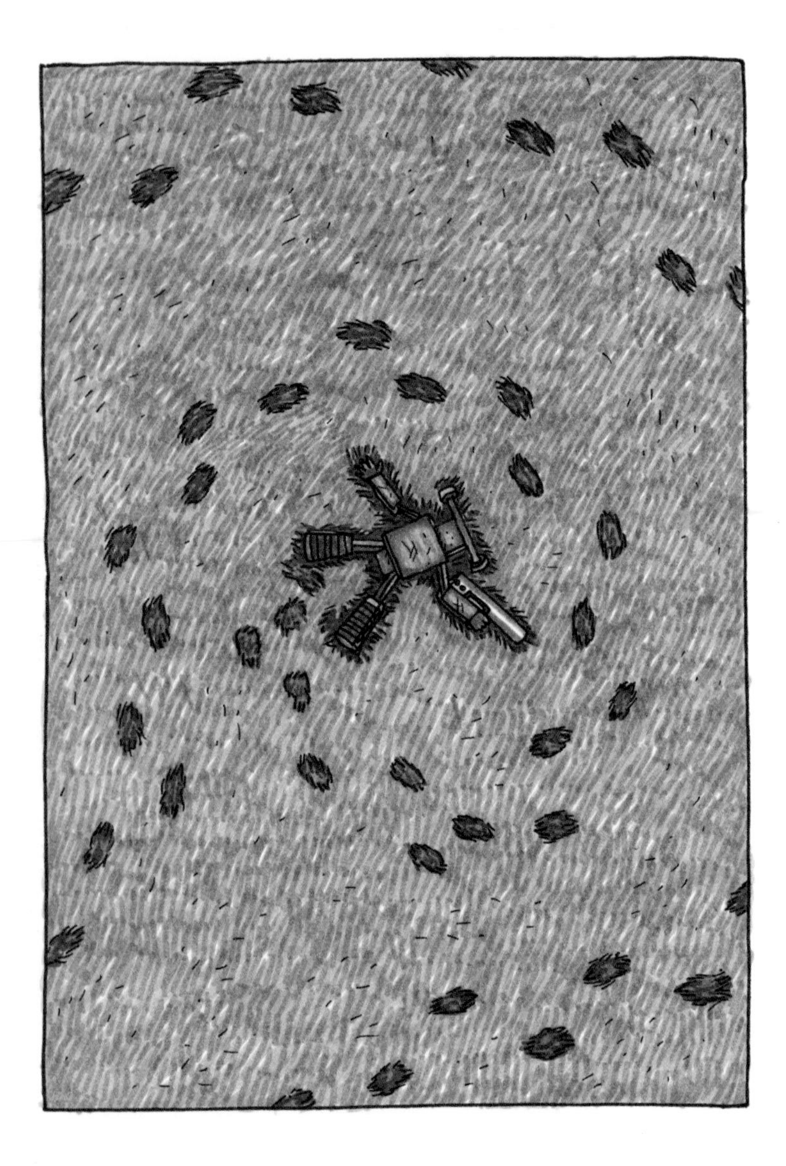

Shootertron
Dairy Diary

Edna says I should try writing a diary and maybe that'll help me remember who I am and stuff. I don't think it's working.
IT'S TOO HARD!
MAYBE YOU'RE RIGHT-HANDED?
Edna and Stanley are taking good care of me though.
THIS'LL FIX YOU UP, BIG GUY.
They even let me have my own room!

Stanley is showing me all about the farm while I regain my strength.
There is something I do not trust about this "tractor"...
I feel Stanley may be in danger.
I'm watching you, "tractor"!

Today Edna was giving me a bath and found something exciting:
OH MY, WILL YOU LOOK AT THAT!
My name!
SHOOTERTRON
Stanley wants to keep calling me "Big Guy"
HEY BIG GUY
But Edna and I think maybe hearing my name will help trigger my memory. Watch out world, "Shootertron" is coming back!

Stanley and I have found lots of ways for me to help out on the farm.

The work is easy for me, but I have begun to feel uneasy. Like I'm missing something.

Maybe I should go on some kind of adventure.

SIGH.

Last night I had a horrifying experience.

Loud noises woke me up...

CHEE CHOOCHEE CHOO CHOOK

I opened my eyes and it looked like the walls were all closing in on me.

I tried to move, but I couldn't!

Eventually I must have passed out.

In the morning I felt normal again. Was it all just a bad dream?

Edna thinks I've been bored, so she enrolled me in the local high school.
OOH! OOH!
I'M getting all kinds of different grades. I think I've gotten almost all of them!
C
D
A-
B+
I've also started playing in the football team. Coach says I've got lots of potential.

This morning was amazing--Stanley was attacked by Tracktor!
OH NO, THE BRAKE!
I was too far away to help, so I just threw out my hands and yelled "Noooooo!"
NOOOOOOO!
And guess what: I stopped Tracktor!
RAZOW!
Stanley looked at me with an expression that could only be one thing: Pride.

I've always felt different from Edna and Stanley, but my new power makes me feel this more keenly than ever.
I don't want to make Edna and Stanley jealous, so I'm careful to practice secretly late at night.
RAZOW!
RAZOW!
This power is totally the best thing ever!

More good news! I've taken the presidency of the Junior class!
Even the guy running against me voted for me. It helped that I applied everything I've been learning in school.
I feel like I'm on top of the world!
AS YOUR PRESIDENT, I PROMISE TO LEAD YOU TO VICTORY!
EEEEEEEEEEEEEEEE
FEEDBACK!

More bad dreams last night.
ARGGHH!
I think my past is coming back to me, and I'm afraid of who I may be...
HA HA HA HA HA!
...or who I was. I know inside I'm a good person, just like Stanley and Edna say.
There's something else, something Stanley and Edna can't find out if anything happens to me.
So I'm going to start writing in binary form from now on.

AND...? WHAT DOES IT SAY AFTER THAT?
UM, WE'RE NOT SURE EXACTLY.
WHAT, YOU GUYS CAN'T TRANSLATE BINARY?
ACTUALLY, WE'RE PRETTY SURE HE DOESN'T REALLY KNOW BINARY.
OH.
YEAH, IT JUST COMES OUT AS A BUNCH OF GOBBLEDYGOOK.
HM. WELL, IT CERTAINLY SEEMS AUTHENTIC. IF SHOOTERTRON REALLY HAS RE-SURFACED, THE GOVERNMENT MUST STOP AT NOTHING TO BRING HIM UNDER OUR CONTROL.

DO WE HAVE VISUAL CONFIRMATION?
NOT YET. WE'VE GOT OUR BEST MEN GOOGLE IMAGE SEARCHING NOW...
BUT WE DO HAVE AN EYEWITNESS. SHOOTERTRON'S ARCH-RIVAL, WHO BROUGHT US THE DIARY.
OH, THAT'S HIM?
YES... WHY?
ER, I JUST IMAGINED HIM BEING A WHITE GUY FOR SOME REASON. SORRY.
SO, TELL US, WHAT DOES THIS "SHOOTERTRON" LOOK LIKE?
WELL, HE'S A BIG METAL GUY, AND-
LIKE, SILVER METAL?
UM, MORE GRAYISH.
BUT SHINY?
WELL, I MEAN..

NEVER MIND. DOES HE HAVE A LONG PIPE ON HIS HEAD, AND A BIG PIPE ON HIS ARM? LOTS OF PIPES?
UM, YEAH. THAT SOUNDS LIKE HIM.
WE CAN'T WAIT FOR FURTHER EVIDENCE. WE MUST ACT NOW.
WAIT, WHAT'RE YOU GOING TO DO? I WAS TOLD HE WOULDN'T BE HURT!
IT'S NONE OF YOUR CONCERN.
THAT WASN'T THE DEAL!
TAKE HIM AWAY.
YOU'LL STILL PAY FOR MY COLLEGE, RIGHT?
YES... AFTER YOU'VE SERVED, OF COURSE.
WHAT?! THIS IS A SCAM!
WELL, THAT ALMOST GOT REALLY AWKWARD. ANYWAY, SEND AGENT RECOG. IF HE CAN'T CONVINCE SHOOTERTRON TO COME PEACEFULLY...

"...WE'LL BRING HIM IN BY FORCE!"
DARD FARMS
WHAT IS IT?
GO TO YOUR ROOM, BIG GUY. I'LL TAKE CARE OF THIS.
MR. DARD? I'M FROM THE GOVERNMENT. I NEED TO TALK TO YOU.
NO THANK YOU.
MR. DARD, WE KNOW YOU'VE BEEN HOUSING A... ROBOT. WE'RE HERE TO TAKE HIM TO A BETTER PLACE.
NO THANKS

MR. DARD, THIS ROBOT IS EXTREMELY DANGEROUS. LET ME SHOW YOU... NOW, THIS MAY BE DISTURBING.
I DON'T WANT TO SEE.
MR. DARD, JUST LET ME SHOW YOU THIS FOOTAGE OF WHAT YOUR ROBOT HAS BEEN UP TO.
LOOK, MISTER.
VERY WELL, MR. DARD. BUT THIS ISN'T THE END OF THIS!
STANLEY, WHAT'S HAPPENING? WHAT'S HAPPENING, STANLEY?
WE'VE GOT SOME WORK TO DO, BIG GUY. THEY'LL BE BACK.

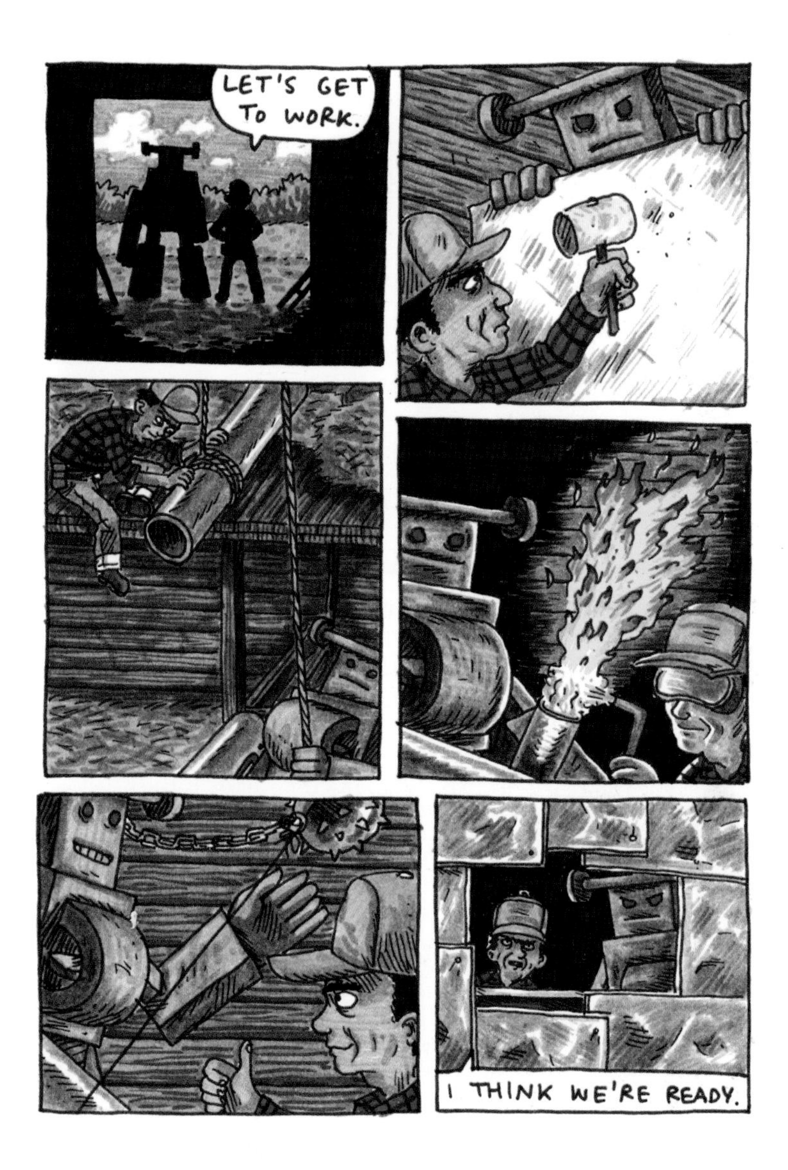
LET'S GET TO WORK.
I THINK WE'RE READY.

CRASH
KLANG
WHIRRRRRRRRRRR
HOW DID YOU DEFEAT US SO EASILY?
WE'VE HAD YOU UNDER SURVEILLANCE FOR WEEKS, AS YOU PREPARED YOUR LITTLE FORTRESS, ANALYZING WEAKNESSES AND PROBABLE SCENARIOS THE WHOLE TIME USING THE--
OKAY, OKAY
AND WE'RE ALSO AMONGST THE--
OKAY! SERIOUSLY WE GET IT.

WE'RE IN TROUBLE... THESE GUYS AREN'T JUST FROM THE GOVERNMENT.
THAT'S RIGHT. WE'RE FROM A WASHINGTON THINK TANK!
OWW!
STANLEY! HIS HEART!
STANLEY! NOOO!
I WILL AVENGE YOU, STANLEY!
WHAT ARE YOU TALKING ABOUT? I'M FINE.
IT'S JUST THESE CUFFS.
STILL. I WILL AVENGE YOU.
I'D REALLY RATHER YOU DIDN'T.
MAYBE.
WE'LL SEE.

WHERE ARE YOU TAKING HIM?
LOOK, MR. DARD. THIS ROBOT BEING IS POSSIBLY THE MOST POWERFUL WEAPON ON EARTH, SO--
DUDE, SHUT UP.
SO, UH, DON'T WORRY ABOUT IT.
YEAH, JUST TRUST US.
UH...
LET ME GUESS. THEY DIDN'T TELL YOU WHERE THEY WERE GOING EITHER.
YEAH, NOT EXACTLY.
I DON'T THINK THEY LIKE ME.

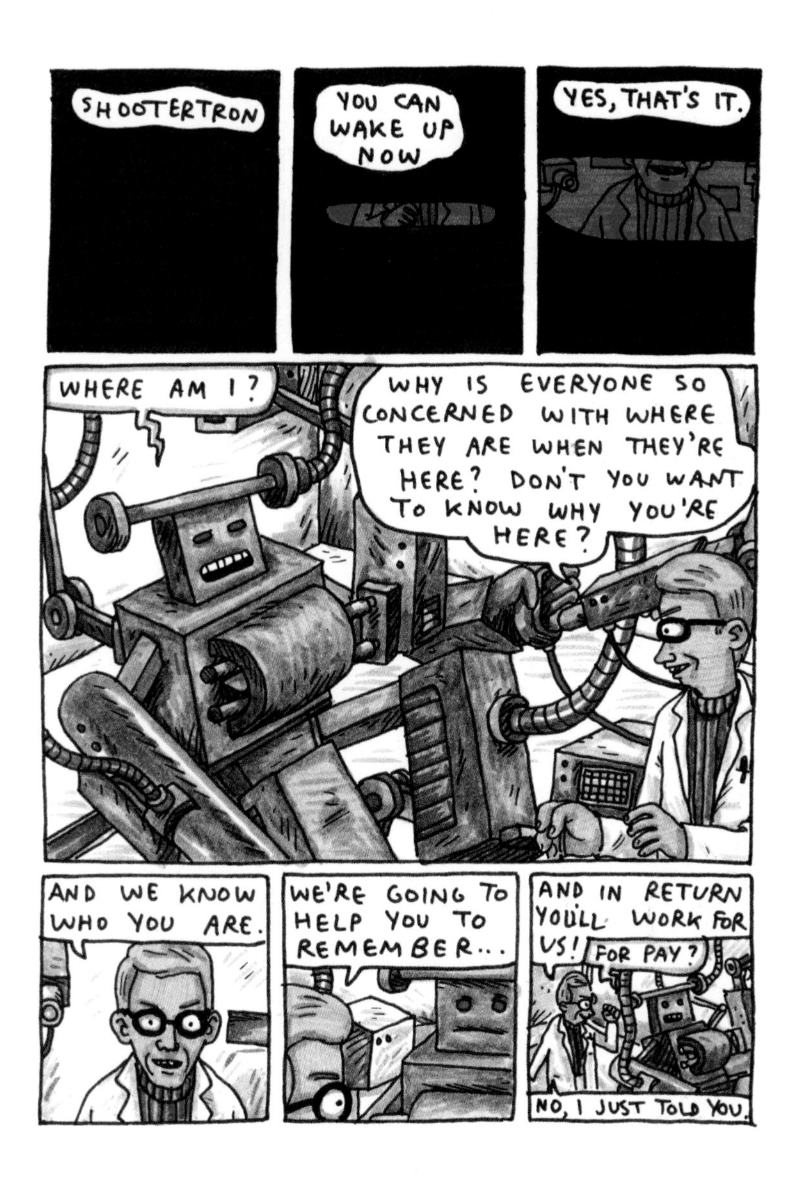
SHOOTERTRON
YOU CAN WAKE UP NOW
YES, THAT'S IT.
WHERE AM I?
WHY IS EVERYONE SO CONCERNED WITH WHERE THEY ARE WHEN THEY'RE HERE? DON'T YOU WANT TO KNOW WHY YOU'RE HERE?
AND WE KNOW WHO YOU ARE.
WE'RE GOING TO HELP YOU TO REMEMBER...
AND IN RETURN YOU'LL WORK FOR US!
FOR PAY?
NO, I JUST TOLD YOU.

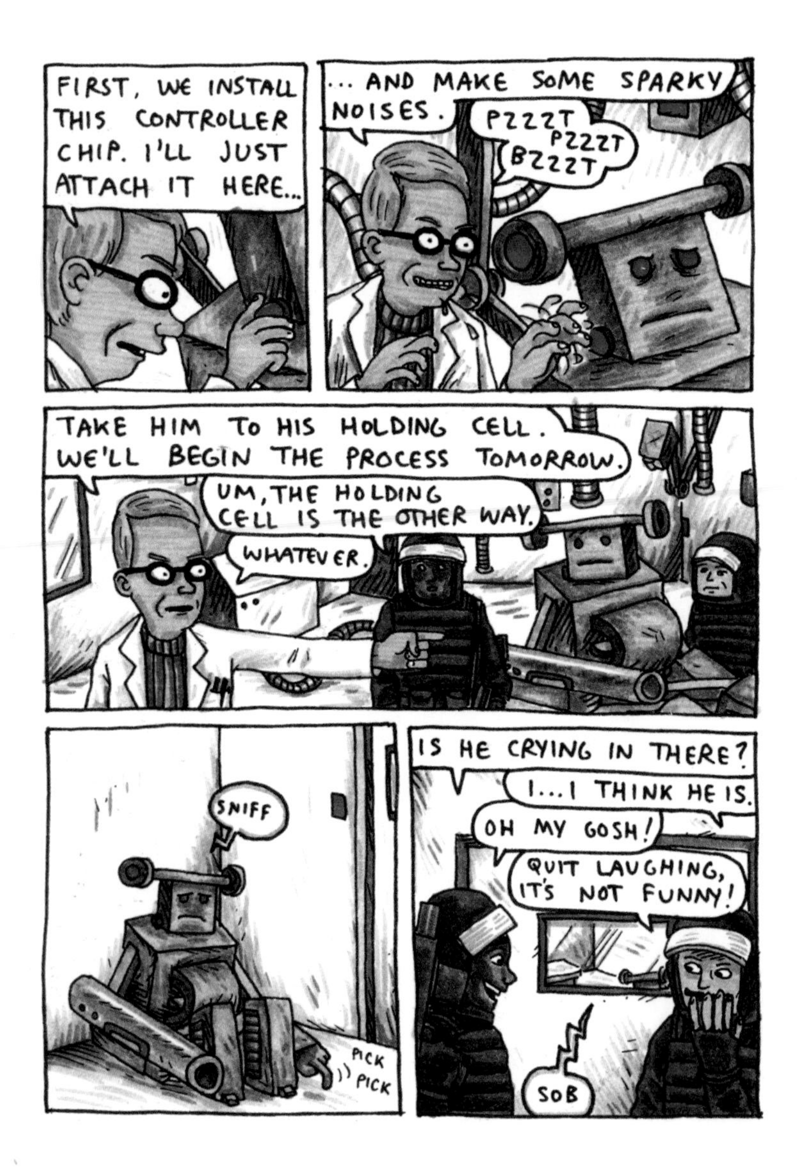
FIRST, WE INSTALL THIS CONTROLLER CHIP. I'LL JUST ATTACH IT HERE...
... AND MAKE SOME SPARKY NOISES.
PZZZT PZZZT BZZZT
TAKE HIM TO HIS HOLDING CELL. WE'LL BEGIN THE PROCESS TOMORROW.
UM, THE HOLDING CELL IS THE OTHER WAY.
WHATEVER.
SNIFF
PICK PICK
IS HE CRYING IN THERE?
I...I THINK HE IS.
OH MY GOSH!
QUIT LAUGHING, IT'S NOT FUNNY!
SOB

NOW, SHOOT THE TARGET!
NO, I CAN'T.
CLICK
SHOOOTT IT!
NO! I CAN'T DO IT!
NGGGHH
SOB
I KNOW, IT'S HARD. JUST SHOOT THE TARGET. JUST A LITTLE.
FOR ME? SHOOT IT A LITTLE?
NO, NEVER!
JUST A TEENY TINY BIT?
NEVERRRRR!

HOW GOES THE TESTING, DOCTOR?
SLOWLY.
SHOOTERTRON SEEMS TO OPERATE WITH A WARM, GENTLE EFFICIENCY RATHER THAN A COLD AND RUTHLESS ONE!
SLAM!
WE NEED OUR WEAPON, DOCTOR. YOU PROMISED!
SLAM!
WELL, IT'S HARD. YOU WON'T EVEN LET ME DO A DOUBLE BLIND STUDY ON THIS!
SLAM!
I NEED MORE TIME!
WE NEED OUR WEAPON NOW!
SLAM!
SLAM!
SLAM!
DOES YOUR HAND HURT? MINE KIND OF HURTS NOW.
YEAH, A LITTLE.

HE LOOKS ALMOST...
PEACEFUL...
DON'T BE FOOLED, SOLDIER. I KNOW SHOOTERTRON WELL. THE HUGE GUN HE CARRIES IS NO METAPHOR.
IF WE CAN CONTROL HIM, THOUGH, HE WILL BE ONE OF OUR GREATEST WEAPONS.
AND IF WE CAN'T?
HUH? CAN'T WHAT?
IF WE CAN'T CONTROL HIM... IF WE END UP JUST UNLEASHING HIM UPON THE WORLD.
OH, RIGHT.
IN THAT CASE, WE'LL SIMPLY USE HIM FOR TECHNICAL RESEARCH BY DISMANTLING HIM. OR SOMETHING SIMILARLY HORRIFIC.

LOOK, SHOOTERTRON. I KNOW THIS IS HARD, AND CONFUSING. I'VE BEEN THERE MYSELF, AND I -- HOLD ON. YES? OH? UH-HUNH... SORRY ABOUT THAT. YEP. OKAY. HA! YEP, THANKS. OKAY, SORRY. ALRIGHT! YEP. BYE.
SORRY, I'M SUPPOSED TO BE "BAD COP." SO, SHOOTERTRON, IF YOU CAN'T SHOOT THE TARGET, PERHAPS I WILL.
UMM...
YEAH, I KNOW.
SORRY, I CAN'T HELP THINKING OF YOU AS "GOOD COP" NOW.
SIGH.

I AM GOING TO KILL YOU! AND THEN I'M GOING TO KILL YOUR FAMILIES! AND THEN YOUR FAMILIES' FRIENDS, AND THEN THEIR FRIENDS' RELATIVES!
YES! THAT'S IT, GIVE YOURSELF TO YOUR ANGER!
YOU'RE JUST JOKING, AREN'T YOU?
YEAH.
HEH HEH
YEAHHHHHH...
HMMMM.
HM.

TWITCH
TWITCH
SHOOTERTRON!
SHOOTERTRON!
BEW!
BEW!
SHOOTERTRON
SHOOTERTRON--
SHOOTERTRON!
I...
...I REMEMBER.

MEANWHILE, IN SPACE

HOW GOES OUR JOURNEY...
...BALLS?*
* NOTICE HOW DRAMATIC REVEALING OF BALLS HEIGHTENS EXCITEMENT OF EXPERIENCE FOR READERS FAMILIAR WITH BALLS
IT GOES WELL SHORTLY WE'LL BE APPROACHING JUPITER...
USING ITS GRAVITY TO INCREASE SPEED AND ESCAPE FROM THE EARTH SOLAR SYSTEM.
NICE SIMULATION
THANKS
GREAT. I'M GOING TO CHECK ON IVY'S PROGRESS.
OKAY. I'M JUST GOING TO SIT HERE.

HOW ARE THE REPAIRS COMING ALONG, IVY?
I'M MAKING PROGRESS, BIG RIG, DESPITE THE LIMITED SUPPLIES WE HAVE TO WORK WITH.
SPARKY HAS BEEN LOTS OF HELP.
UM...
YEAH. I'M JUST A HEAD.
BUT HE CAN STILL INCREDIBLE CHANGE INTO FULL VEHICLE FORM.
YEAH, GREAT. I CAN CHANGE FROM A JET INTO A HEAD. SWEET!
JUST THINK, THOUGH, AFTERBURNERBOT. YOU CAN'T WALK... BUT YOU CAN FLY!

AS YOU CAN SEE, THERE'S STILL SOME WORK TO DO.
MEDIOCRE CHANGE!
CHEE
CHOO
CHOOK
WAIT, WHO IS THIS?
IT'S ME, HOSER!
INCREDIBLE CHANGE!
CHE
CHEE
CHOO
OH.
I GOT A WHOLE NEW REDESIGN!
AND, I'VE GIVEN THEM SOME PRIVACY, BUT I'VE MANAGED TO REBUILD THESE TWO...
AWWWWWWW!
SHHH!

I'M SO GLAD YOU'RE BACK, HONKYTONK. I LOVE YOU SO MUCH IT HURTS...
YEAH, IT HURTS. IT HURTS ME!
I SAID I WAS SORRY!
YEAH, BUT YOU DIDN'T SAY IT LIKE YOU MEANT IT!
I'M A ROBOT. EVERYTHING I SAY SOUNDS THE SAME.
I KNOW, SIREN...
I JUST NEED TIME.
WE'LL WORK THROUGH THIS, OKAY?
KLINK
KLANK
KLINK

VERY WELL. YOU SHOULD COME TO THE CONCLAVE LATER. IN THE MEANTIME, KEEP UP THE GOOD WORK.
IT MUST BE VERY SATISFYING TO PLAY GOD.
IS THAT WHAT I'M DOING? PLAYING GOD?
IS IT ETHICAL TO MODIFY AND MANIPULATE THESE CHANGE-BOTS? IS IT IMMORAL TO PLAY GOD?
BUT, IF I WERE GOD... I'D GET TO DECIDE WHAT'S MORAL OR ETHICAL!
OKAY, BACK TO WORK!

LATER, AT THE CONCLAVE
THANK YOU ALL FOR COMING. I'M HONORED TO HAVE LED YOU ALL SINCE LEAVING EARTH, BUT I AM ONCE AGAIN CONSIDERING STEPPING DOWN...
I'M COMING UPON YET ANOTHER ANNIVERSARY OF MY DATE OF MANUFACTURE, SO---
WE ALL HAVE THE SAME DATE OF MANUFACTURE, THOUGH.
YEAH, WHAT'S THAT HAVE TO DO WITH ANYTHING?
THANK YOU, WHEEEEE. ANYWAY, I'VE BEEN THINKING ABOUT IT, AND I'VE DECIDED THERE'S A BETTER OPTION THAN ME LEADING...
LET'S HEAR HIM OUT, FELLOW CHANGE-BOTS!
FINALLY, MY CHANCE TO STEP IN AND LEAD!

I THINK WE SHOULD HAVE A RULING COUNCIL OF THREE CHANGE-BOTS; ONE FORMER AWESOMEBOT, ONE FORMER FANTASTICON, AND MYSELF.
YES! AND I-- WAIT, WHAT?
I NOMINATE EJECT AND RUSTY TO JOIN ME ON THE COUNCIL.
YES!
THAT SOUNDS GOOD.
GREAT IDEA, BIG RIG!
THIS WILL BE GREAT.
WOW, WHY DIDN'T WE THINK OF THIS BEFORE?
RULING TOGETHER, IT MAKES SO MUCH SENSE!
I HATE TO INTERRUPT, BUT I HAVE BAD NEWS... IT SEEMS OUR TRAJECTORY HAS BEEN MISCALCULATED!
BURST!
WE'RE GOING TO CRASH BACK ON EARTH!

HOW COULD THIS HAPPEN? YOU TRIPLE CHECKED THE NUMBERS, RIGHT?
UM...YEAH. WELL, I MEAN, A FEW TIMES.
A FEW?
YEAH, A FEW. TWO TIMES. YOU SAID "CHECK A FEW TIMES."
"A FEW" IS THREE.
I THOUGHT "SEVERAL" WAS THREE.
THEY BOTH ARE. "A COUPLE" IS TWO.
OH.
I DON'T UNDERSTAND, CALCULATRON... YOU SAID WE COULD COUNT ON YOU!
YEAH...
HEH HEH
OH, I GET IT.

THE PROBLEM WITH YOU GUYS IS THAT YOU'RE FAILURES AT EVERYTHING YOU DO!
HOW ABOUT THIS, IS THIS A FAILURE?
KLANG!
OW!
HUH? WAS THAT A FAILURE?
FLINCH
I DON'T KNOW, RACEY, WHAT WERE YOU TRYING TO DO?

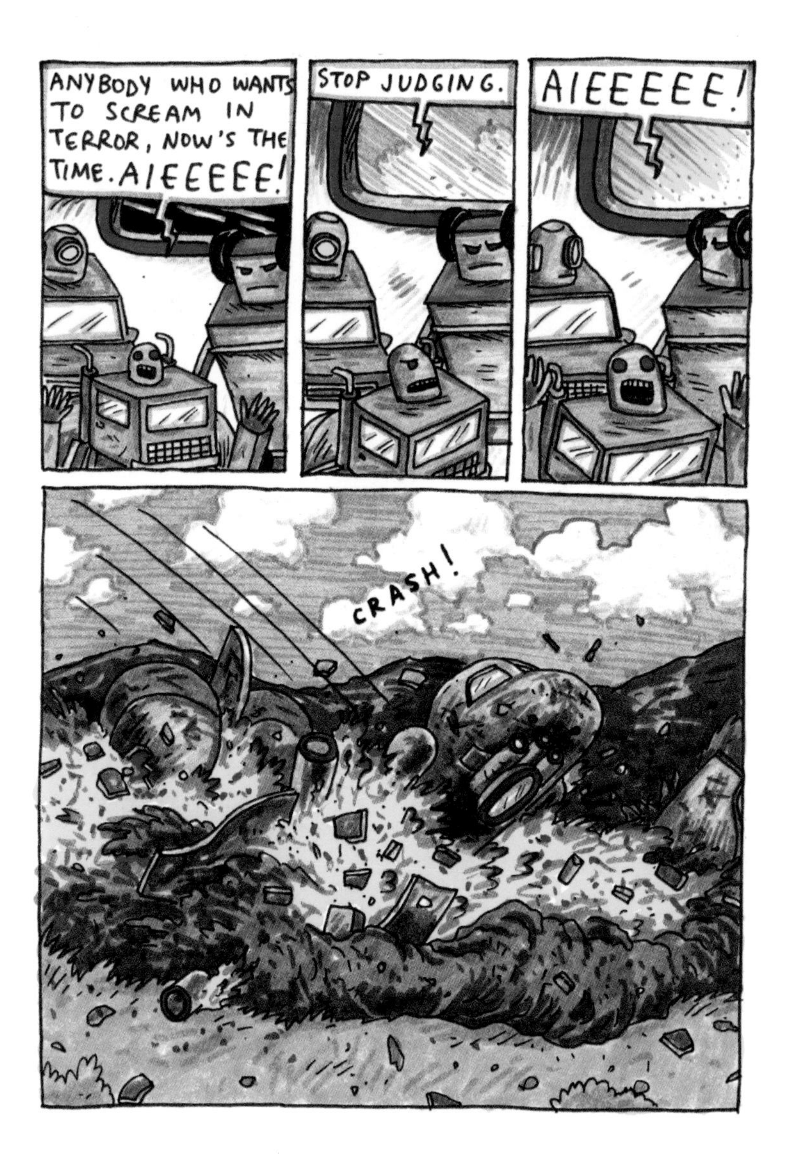
ANYBODY WHO WANTS TO SCREAM IN TERROR, NOW'S THE TIME. AIEEEEE!
STOP JUDGING.
AIEEEEEE!
CRASH!

HM, THAT WASN'T SO BAD.
YEAH. EVERYONE OKAY?
YEAH.
WELL, I GUESS WE'LL NEED TO... TALK TO SOMEONE? TELL THEM WE'RE HERE?
YEAH, MAYBE WE SHOULD INCREDIBLE CHANGE TO VEHICLE MODE. PUT THEM MORE AT EASE.
INCREDIBLE CHANGE!
CHEE CHOO CHUK
INCREDIBLE CHANGE!
CHU CHE CHUK
INCREDIBLE CHANGE!
INCREDIBLE CHANGE!
INCREDIBLE CHANGE!
CHEE
CHEE CHOO
CHOO CHEE CHUK
INCREDIBLE CHANGE!
INCREDIBLE CHANGE!
OKAY, EVERYONE CAN LOAD UP INTO MY NEW CAR TRANSPORTER TRAILER!

OH, HOLD ON-
INCREDIBLE CHANGE!
CHEE
CHOO
CHUK
UH...
UH-OH
KLANG!
OH GREAT, THANKS DOZER. YOU TOTALLY SCREWED UP MY TRAILER!
THIS THING WAS BRAND NEW.
CUT ME SOME SLACK, I'M STILL WORKING OUT MY KINKS.
OKAY, LET'S CALM DOWN. WE'RE ALL A LITTLE STRESSED HERE...
I'M NOT.
LOOK, WHY DON'T WE SEND EXTRA BATTLE DAMAGED ARSONAL AND AFTERBURNERBOT OUT TO SCOUT, WHILE THE REST OF US SET UP A BASE HERE.

WHAT'S THE DAMAGE TO OUR SHIP, CEMENTOR?
THE DAMAGE IS EXTENSIVE, STINKY. WE'LL HAVE TO REBUILD ALMOST FROM SCRATCH.
OH NO!
I WONDER IF NOW IS A GOOD TIME TO TELL THEM THIS ESSENTIAL PART IS IRREPLACEABLE? MMM, IT CAN WAIT.
BIG RIG, WHAT IF IT WAS FATE THAT BROUGHT US BACK HERE?
THINK ABOUT ALL THE COINCIDENCES IT TOOK TO GET US HERE... PERHAPS THIS WAS MEANT TO BE OUR NEW HOME!
NO, I'M PRETTY SURE IT WAS INCOMPETENCE, NOT FATE.
OUCH, DUDE. THAT WAS HARSH.

MEANWHILE, AT A SECRET GOVERNMENT FACILITY...
KEEP OUT
SO DOCTOR, YOU BELIEVE YOU'RE MAKING PROGRESS, DESPITE THE FACT THAT ABSOLUTELY NOTHING HAS CHANGED?
YES, GENERAL. THERE IS MUCH WE CAN STILL LEARN FROM THIS LACK OF CHANGE.
IT STILL REMAINS TO BE SEEN WHETHER ENGINEERING OR PROGRAMMING PLAYS A BIGGER ROLE IN WHO A CHANGE-BOT IS...
AND I THINK I MAY NOW KNOW HOW TO BREAK THROUGH SHOOTERTRON'S DEFENSES.
OOPS! STUPID ROLLY CHAIRS.

EEEE EEEE EEEE EEEE EEEE
ATTENTION! THIS IS NOT A DRILL!
PRISONER S-H-ONE-T-R HAS ESCAPED!
HE IS FULLY ARMED AND FUNCTIONING!
PLEASE REMAIN CALM, AND--
RAZOW! RAZOW! AGGHHH!
KRKKKTTTT
SEE? IT WORKED!

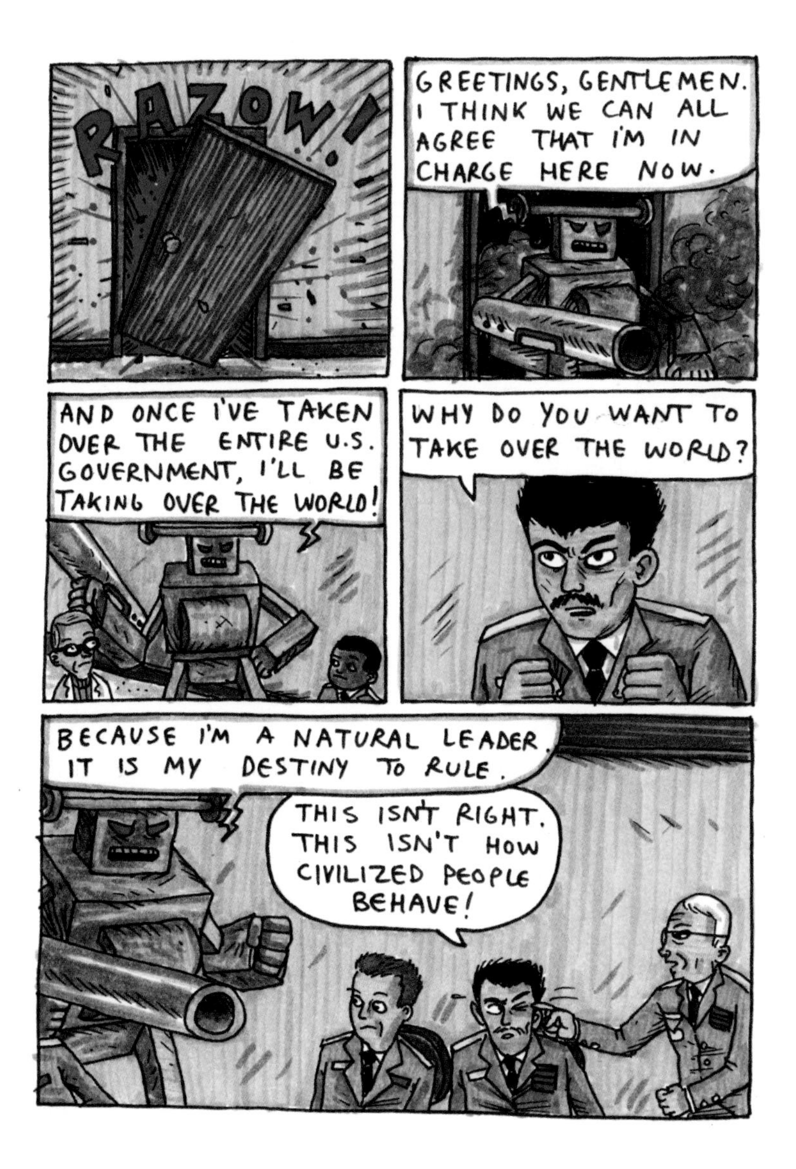
RAZOW!
GREETINGS, GENTLEMEN. I THINK WE CAN ALL AGREE THAT I'M IN CHARGE HERE NOW.
AND ONCE I'VE TAKEN OVER THE ENTIRE U.S. GOVERNMENT, I'LL BE TAKING OVER THE WORLD!
WHY DO YOU WANT TO TAKE OVER THE WORLD?
BECAUSE I'M A NATURAL LEADER. IT IS MY DESTINY TO RULE.
THIS ISN'T RIGHT. THIS ISN'T HOW CIVILIZED PEOPLE BEHAVE!

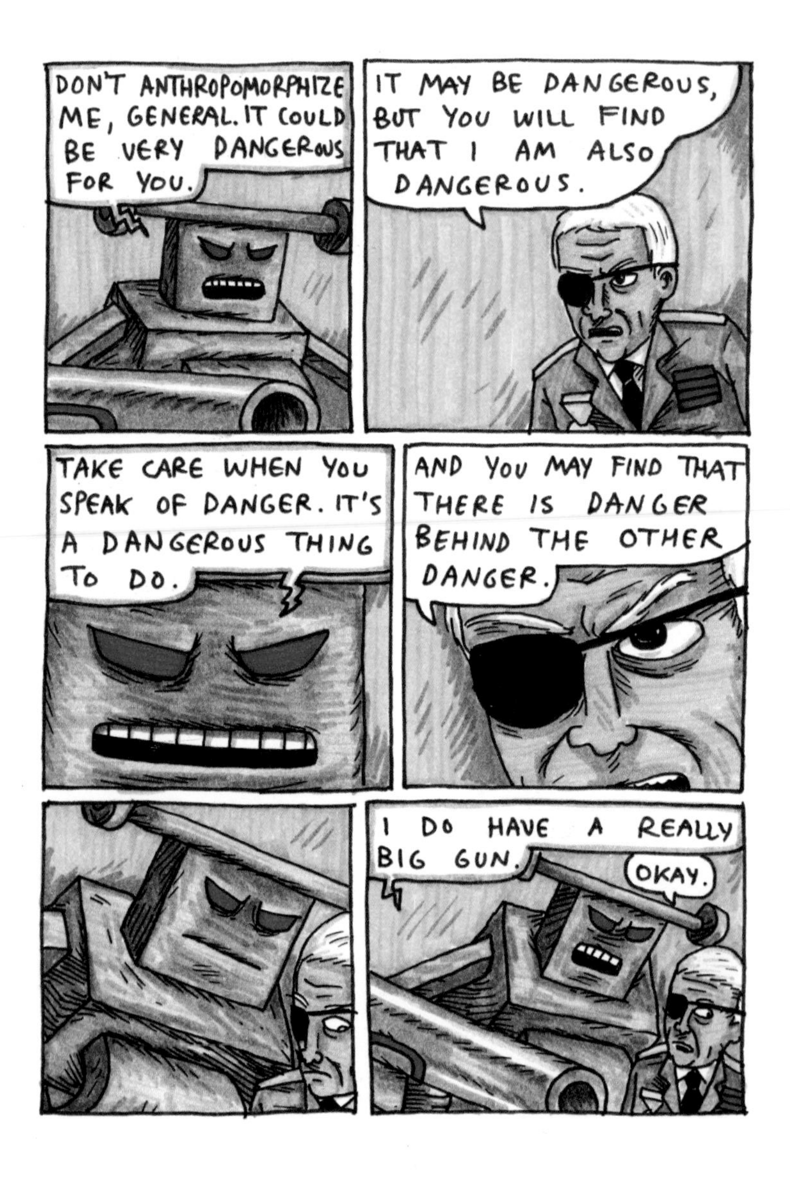
DON'T ANTHROPOMORPHIZE ME, GENERAL. IT COULD BE VERY DANGEROUS FOR YOU.
IT MAY BE DANGEROUS, BUT YOU WILL FIND THAT I AM ALSO DANGEROUS.
TAKE CARE WHEN YOU SPEAK OF DANGER. IT'S A DANGEROUS THING TO DO.
AND YOU MAY FIND THAT THERE IS DANGER BEHIND THE OTHER DANGER.
I DO HAVE A REALLY BIG GUN.
OKAY.

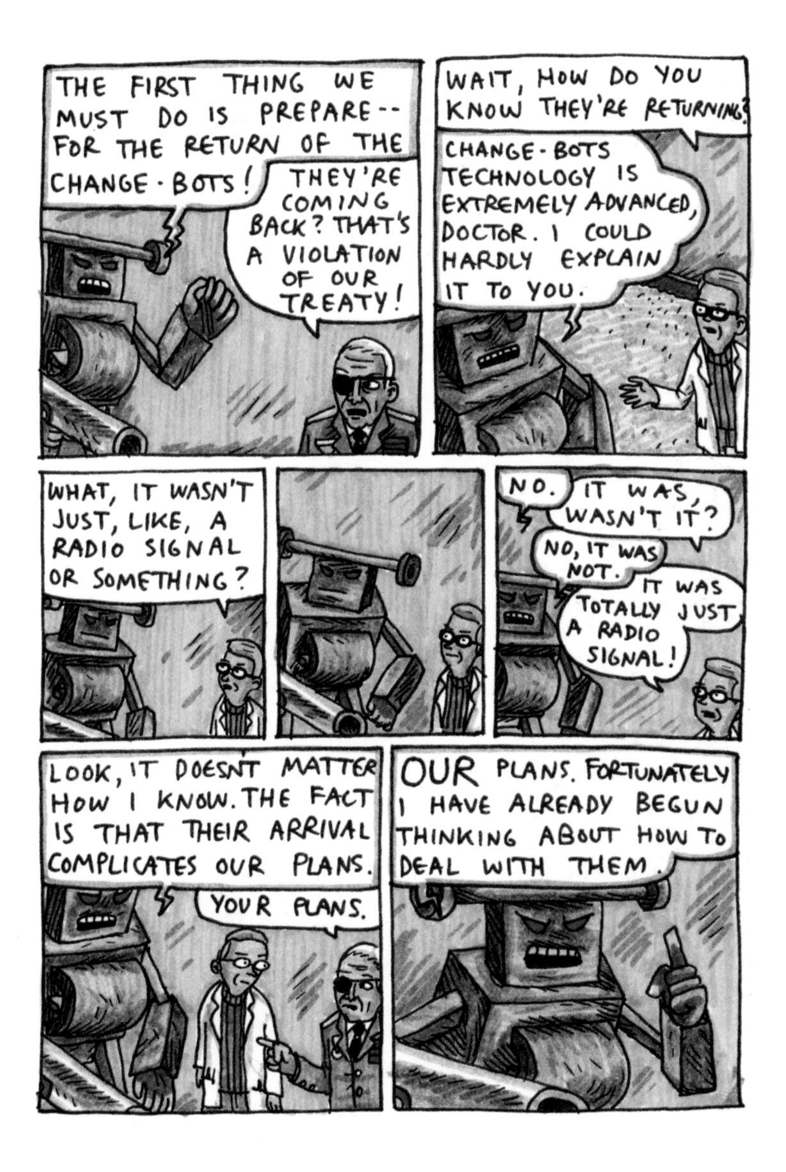
THE FIRST THING WE MUST DO IS PREPARE-- FOR THE RETURN OF THE CHANGE-BOTS!
THEY'RE COMING BACK? THAT'S A VIOLATION OF OUR TREATY!
WAIT, HOW DO YOU KNOW THEY'RE RETURNING?
CHANGE-BOTS TECHNOLOGY IS EXTREMELY ADVANCED, DOCTOR. I COULD HARDLY EXPLAIN IT TO YOU.
WHAT, IT WASN'T JUST, LIKE, A RADIO SIGNAL OR SOMETHING?
NO.
IT WAS, WASN'T IT?
NO, IT WAS NOT.
IT WAS TOTALLY JUST A RADIO SIGNAL!
LOOK, IT DOESN'T MATTER HOW I KNOW. THE FACT IS THAT THEIR ARRIVAL COMPLICATES OUR PLANS.
YOUR PLANS.
OUR PLANS. FORTUNATELY I HAVE ALREADY BEGUN THINKING ABOUT HOW TO DEAL WITH THEM.

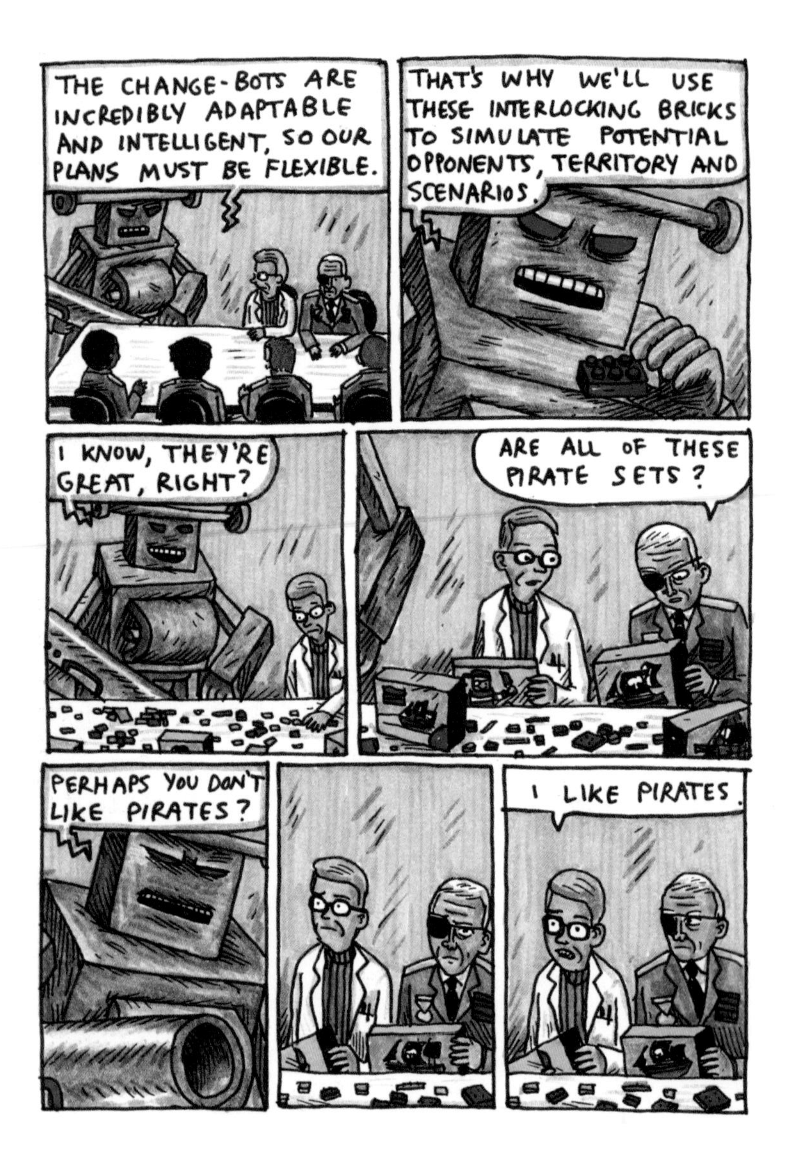
THE CHANGE-BOTS ARE INCREDIBLY ADAPTABLE AND INTELLIGENT, SO OUR PLANS MUST BE FLEXIBLE.
THAT'S WHY WE'LL USE THESE INTERLOCKING BRICKS TO SIMULATE POTENTIAL OPPONENTS, TERRITORY AND SCENARIOS.
I KNOW, THEY'RE GREAT, RIGHT?
ARE ALL OF THESE PIRATE SETS?
PERHAPS YOU DON'T LIKE PIRATES?
I LIKE PIRATES.

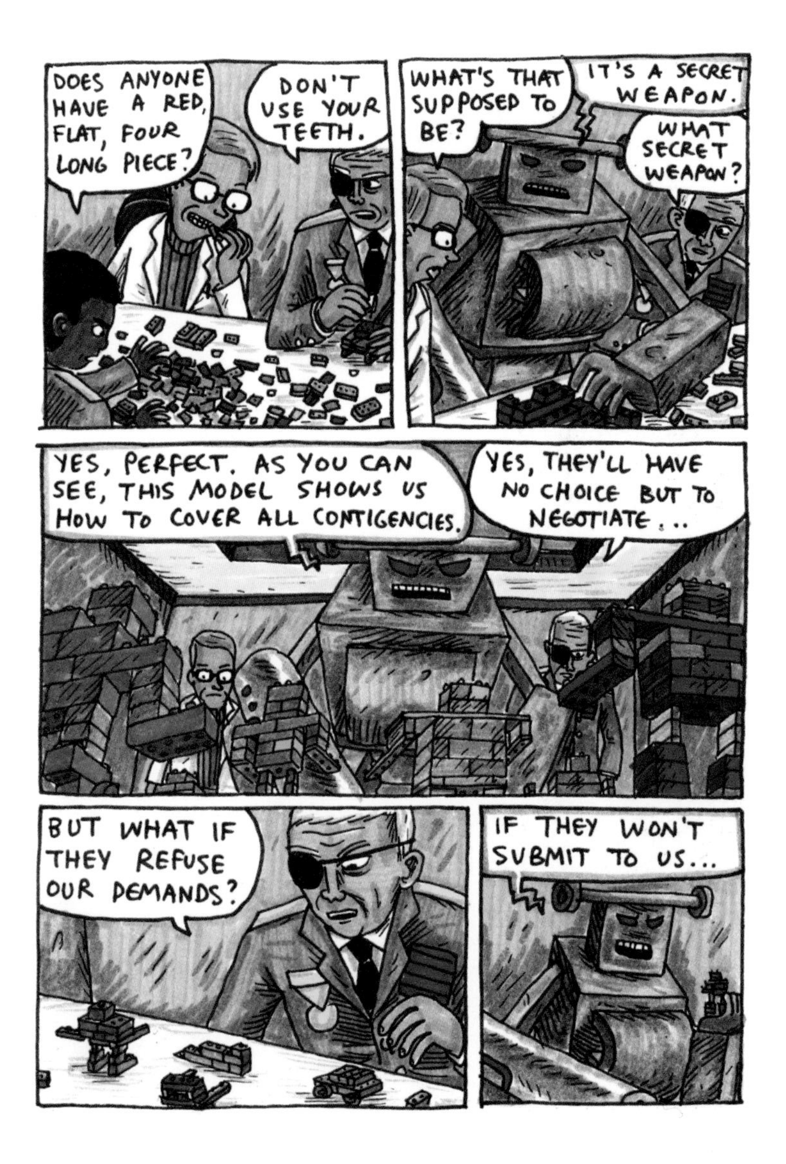

DOES ANYONE HAVE A RED, FLAT, FOUR LONG PIECE?
DON'T USE YOUR TEETH.
WHAT'S THAT SUPPOSED TO BE?
IT'S A SECRET WEAPON.
WHAT SECRET WEAPON?
YES, PERFECT. AS YOU CAN SEE, THIS MODEL SHOWS US HOW TO COVER ALL CONTIGENCIES.
YES, THEY'LL HAVE NO CHOICE BUT TO NEGOTIATE...
BUT WHAT IF THEY REFUSE OUR DEMANDS?
IF THEY WON'T SUBMIT TO US...

WE WILL EXCAVATE THEM!!
UM... YOU MEAN "EVISCERATE" THEM?
YES, THAT'S WHAT I SAID.
NO, YOU SAID "EXCAVATE."
"EXCAVATE?" I DIDN'T SAY THAT. THAT MAKES NO SENSE.
I SAID "EVISCERATE"
WHATEVER.
DON'T TELL ME WHAT I SAID.

BREAKING NEWS
LIVE
HD

GOOD EVENING. WE'RE INTERRUPTING TONIGHT'S REGULARLY SCHEDULED PROGRAMMING TO BRING YOU A SPECIAL REPORT.
FOR THE PAST THREE YEARS, THERE HAVE BEEN RUMORS OF ALIEN ROBOTS LANDING ON EARTH.
ACCORDING TO THE INTERNET, THE GOVERNMENT COVERED UP THE DESTRUCTION AND CONFLICT THESE ROBOTS LEFT IN THEIR WAKE.
THESE REPORTS WERE LARGELY DISMISSED, BECAUSE THE INTERNET DIDN'T HAVE THE SAME RESPECT AND VALIDATION IT HAS TODAY.
NOW, REPORTS ARE SURFACING OF ANOTHER CRASH LANDING BY AN ALIEN ROBOT SPACECRAFT.

HERE IS AN ARTIST'S CONCEPTION OF A ROBOT BASED ON EYEWITNESS ACCOUNTS
HERE IS AN ARTIST'S CONCEPTION BASED ON SOME REALLY GRAINY VIDEO WE SAW
AND HERE IS AN ARTIST'S CONCEPTION BASED ON HIS OWN IMAGINATIVE IDEAS
ARE THESE THE SAME ROBOTS FROM THREE YEARS AGO? AND WHY ARE THEY HERE? WHAT ARE THEY DOING NOW?
WE CAN ONLY SPECULATE WHILE WE WAIT TO SEE IF THIS IS MERELY MORE SCIENCE FICTION...
...OR IF IT IS INDEED SCIENCE FACTION.

AFTER THE BREAK, WE'LL EXAMINE THOSE EARLY REPORTS OF THESE ALIEN ROBOTS.
"SCIENCE FACTION," CARTER? WHAT THE HECK IS THAT?!
I WAS IMPROVISING.
WELL, IT'S STUPID. WE'RE TRYING TO BREAK THE STORY OF THE CENTURY HERE!
YOU CAN'T CHANGE WHO I AM. YOU KNEW THAT WHEN YOU HIRED ME!
AND I CAN F...
SIR!
SIR! THE PHONES ARE LIGHTING UP! THIS IS OUR HIGHEST RATED SHOW EVER!
IT'S A SHOW ABOUT ALIEN ROBOTS, OF COURSE IT'S GOING TO DO WELL!
I'M A RULE BREAKER.
WE HAVEN'T SAVED THIS WEB SERIES YET, CARTER.

IT LOOKS LIKE THEY'RE ALREADY ESTABLISHING A BASE...
I CAN'T SEE
JUST PUT THOSE THINGS DOWN.
THERE'S BIG RIG. WE SUSPECT HE'S ACTING AS LEADER.
NOTICE THEY'VE ALL GOT LASER GUNS.
WE'LL APPROACH OPENLY, BUT CAUTIOUSLY...
... ONCE WE KNOW WHY THEY'RE BACK, SHOOTERTRON WILL BEGIN PHASE TWO OF THE PLAN.

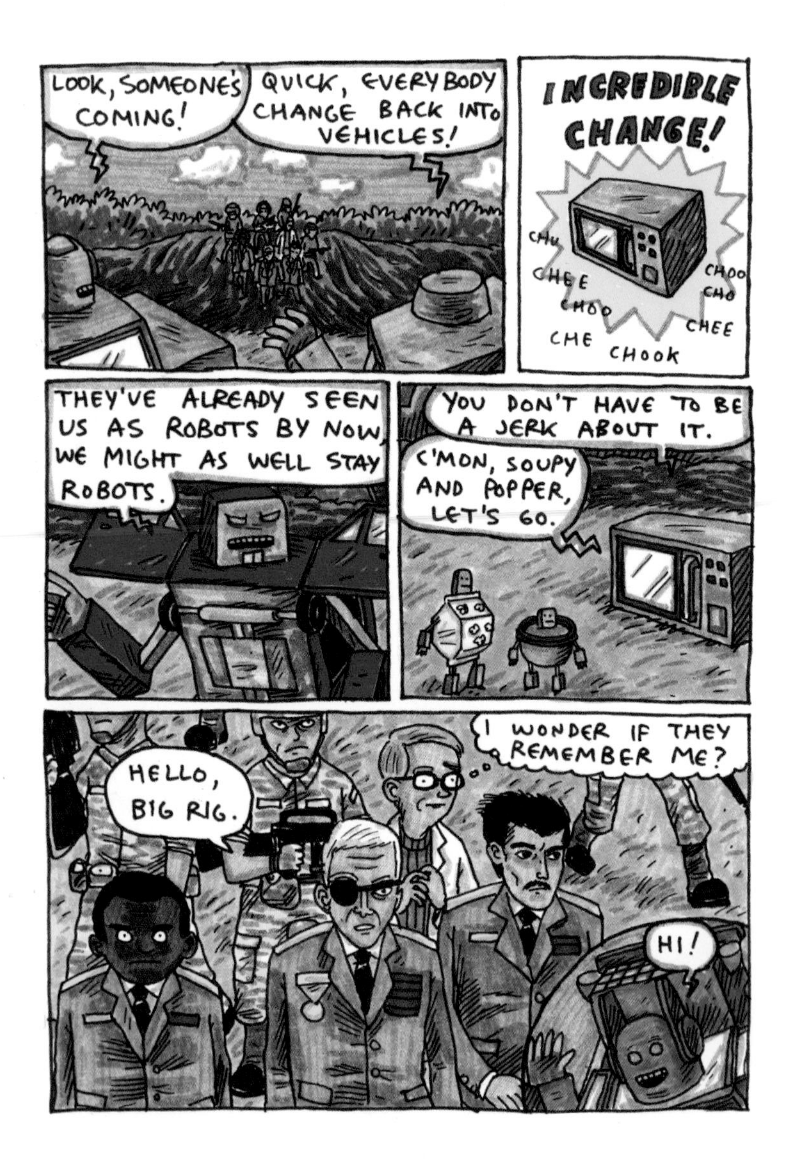
LOOK, SOMEONE'S COMING!
QUICK, EVERYBODY CHANGE BACK INTO VEHICLES!
INCREDIBLE CHANGE!
CHU CHEE CHOO CHE CHOOK CHEE CHO CHOO
THEY'VE ALREADY SEEN US AS ROBOTS BY NOW, WE MIGHT AS WELL STAY ROBOTS.
YOU DON'T HAVE TO BE A JERK ABOUT IT.
C'MON, SOUPY AND POPPER, LET'S GO.
HELLO, BIG RIG.
I WONDER IF THEY REMEMBER ME?
HI!

WHY ARE YOU HERE? THIS VIOLATES OUR TREATY!
YEAH, BUT YOU SEE, WE HAD SOME DIFFICULTIES, AND...
ENOUGH, GENERAL.
IT HARDLY MATTERS WHY THEY'RE HERE.
SHOOTERTRON! YOU'RE BACK!
I'M NOT BACK.
UNLIKE SOME CHANGE-BOTS, I NEVER LEFT.
EXCEPT I LOST MY MEMORY.
SO, IN THAT SENSE IM BACK.
YOU KNOW
BACK TO BEING MYSELF.

AND THAT MEANS YOU HAVE ONLY ONE CHOICE: SUBMIT TO MY AUTHORITY, OR SUFFER THE CONSEQUENCES! SO, TWO CHOICES, ACTUALLY.
GENERAL, YOU'RE WORKING WITH SHOOTERTRON? DIDN'T YOU LEARN YOUR LESSON?
I'M A DREAMER, NOT A NUMBERS GUY, BIGRIG.
DID HE JUST SAY HE'S NOT A NUMBERS GUY?
STOP TALKING TO MY MINIONS! WHAT DO YOU SAY, BROTHER? ARE YOU READY TO SUBMIT TO ME?

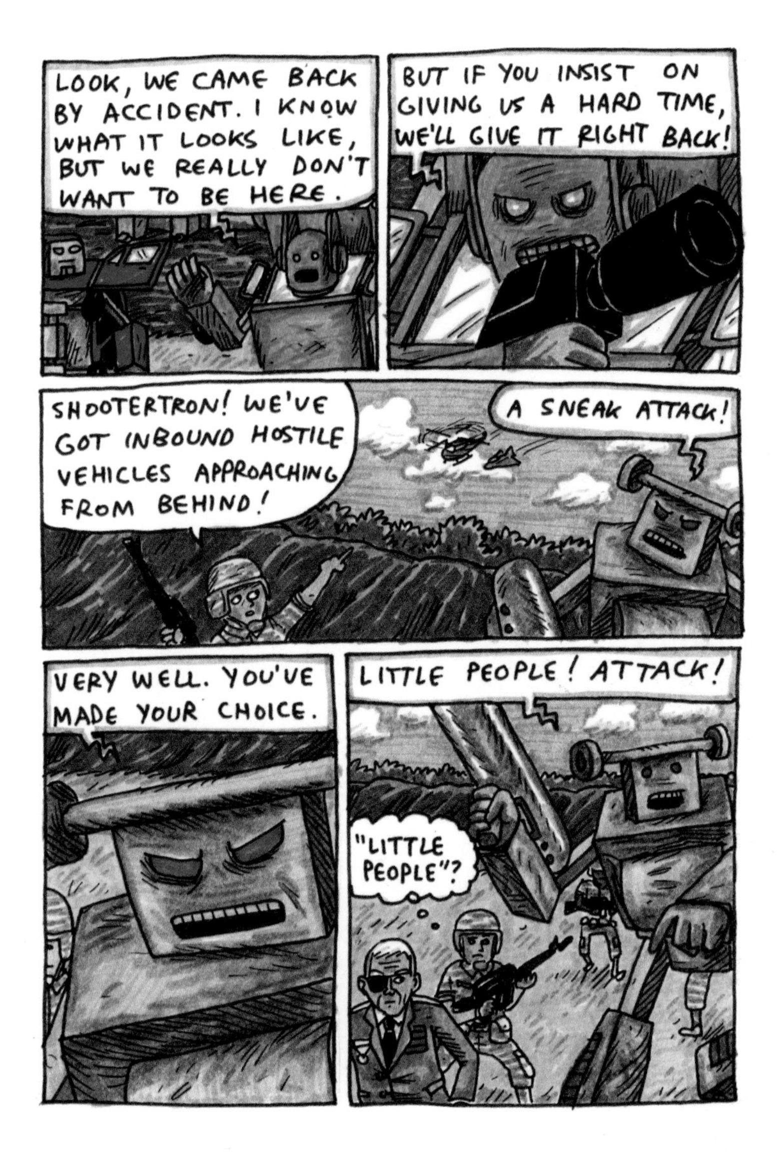
LOOK, WE CAME BACK BY ACCIDENT. I KNOW WHAT IT LOOKS LIKE, BUT WE REALLY DON'T WANT TO BE HERE.
BUT IF YOU INSIST ON GIVING US A HARD TIME, WE'LL GIVE IT RIGHT BACK!
SHOOTERTRON! WE'VE GOT INBOUND HOSTILE VEHICLES APPROACHING FROM BEHIND!
A SNEAK ATTACK!
VERY WELL. YOU'VE MADE YOUR CHOICE.
LITTLE PEOPLE! ATTACK!
"LITTLE PEOPLE"?

FIND COVER AND RETURN FIRE!
POW!
KAPOW!
POW!
BLAM!
KAPOW!
BLAM!
WHOA! HEY!
BLAM!
WHAT'S HAPPENING?
POW!
BLAM!
POW!
BLAM!
KAPOW!
TWINCREDIBLE CHANGE!
CHEE
CHOO
CHU
CHE CHEE
CHOO
CHOOK
CHE
CHEE
CHOO
CHEE
CHO
CHE
CHU
CHEE
CHOO
CHUK
WHAT'S WRONG WITH YOU GUYS? WHY DIDN'T YOU WARN US?
IT'S NOT OUR FAULT!
YEAH, WE PATROLLED THE OTHER DIRECTION.
POW!
BLAW!
BLAM!

UM, BIG RIG, WE'VE GOT A PROBLEM HERE...
WHAT IS IT?
BLAM
BLAM
BEW!
THE HUMAN SOLDIERS HAVE SOME SORT OF TECHNOLOGY THAT ABSORBS OUR LASERS. OUR WEAPONS ARE COMPLETELY INEFFECTIVE... WATCH!
BLAM!
POW!
BEW!
REBEW!
WAIT! HOW IS THAT POSSIBLE? ONLY EJECT HAS ACCESS TO THAT SECRET TECHNOLOGY!
POW!
BLAM!
BLAM!
POW!
BLAM!
POW!
BLAM!
WHAT? I DIDN'T THINK WE WERE COMING BACK HERE. HOW WAS I SUPPOSED TO KNOW?
THEY ASKED NICELY!
POW!
BLAM!
POW!
BLAM!

I THINK IF WE TAKE OUT SHOOTERTRON, THE HUMANS' MORALE WILL BE BROKEN.
AGREED! LET'S DO IT.
NO! I'LL DO IT!
BLAM!
WHY DO YOU ALWAYS HAVE TO DO EVERYTHING YOURSELF?
BLAM!
YEAH, WHY CAN'T YOU BE MORE OF A TEAM PLAYER?
POW!
WHATEVER, I TOTALLY CARRY THIS TEAM...
NOW, YOU GUYS COVER ME, AND YOU GUYS PROVIDE A DISTRACTION WITH A FLANKING MANEUVER.
BLAM!
GO!
POW!
OW!
OW!
BLAM!
BLAM!
BLAM!
OW!
BLAM!
BLAM!
BLAM!
BLAM!
COVERING FIRE! COVERING FIRE!
POW!
POW!

I'M GOING TO HELP!
EXTRA BATTLE DAMAGED ARSONAL, NO! DON'T BE A HERO!
AUGGHH!
HM, THAT'S MORE "MARTYR" THAN "HERO."
BLAM! POW! BLAM! BLAM! BLAM! BLAM! BLAM! POW! BLAM! BLAM! BLAM! POW! BLAM! BLAM!
SO MUCH BEAUTY
AND YET, SO MUCH DESTRUCTION
WHEN WILL IT EVER--
--END?
THAT WAS POETIC.
VERY MOVING.
THE FLOWER WAS A NICE TOUCH.
YEAH.

So, BROTHER, WE MEET AGAIN... BUT THIS TIME, I'VE BEEN PRACTICING!
NO MATTER, MY RIGHTEOUS FURY WILL DESTROY YOU!
YOUR EMOTIONS ARE UNREASONABLE AND ILLOGICAL, BIG RIG.
RA
WRONG! EMOTION IS REALLY A HIGHLY EVOLVED FORM OF LOGIC.
ZOW!
IS THAT SO?
WELL, MY FIST IS A HIGHLY EVOLVED FORM OF LOGIC, TOO!
KLANG!

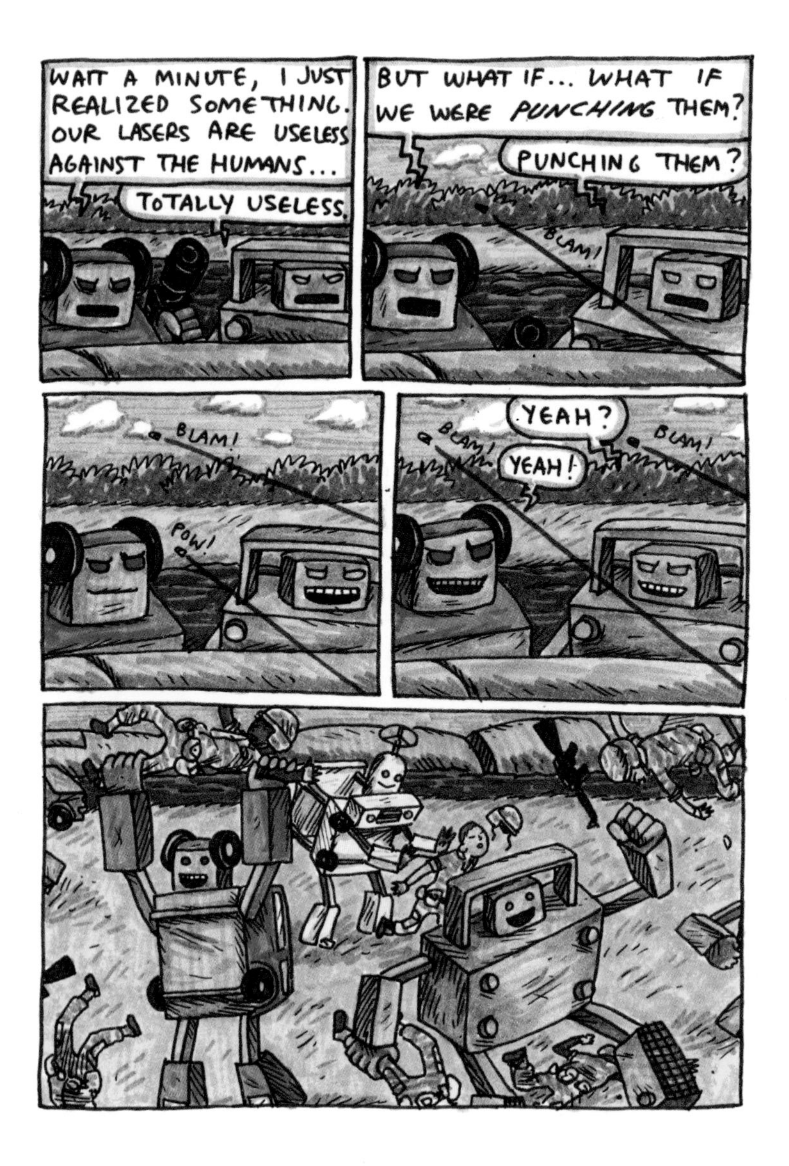
WAIT A MINUTE, I JUST REALIZED SOMETHING. OUR LASERS ARE USELESS AGAINST THE HUMANS...
TOTALLY USELESS.
BUT WHAT IF... WHAT IF WE WERE *PUNCHING* THEM?
PUNCHING THEM?
BLAM!
BLAM!
POW!
BLAM!
YEAH?
YEAH!
BLAM!

WHY ARE YOU SO MEAN, SHOOTERTRON?
I'M NOT MEAN, I'M MISUNDERSTOOD!
KLANG!
WHAT IS THAT SUPPOSED TO MEAN?
YES, EXACTLY.
WHAT? I DON'T GET IT.
OH, I THOUGHT YOU DID.
"MEAN."
HEH HEH
SHOOTERTRON, COME IN, SHOOTERTRON, KCHHHHH
OH, GREAT!
WE'RE, UH, GETTING BEAT PRETTY BADLY HERE, SO WE'RE GOING TO GO AHEAD AND RETREAT

SORRY, BIG RIG, BUT I MUST BE GOING!
SHOVE
UNGH
CRASH!
WHERE DID THIS ALL COME FROM?
THAT WAS US.
WE STARTED MOVING STUFF DURING THE BATTLE.
WE WANTED TO GET A HEAD START.
WOO HOO, THAT WAS AWESOME!
YEAH, DOESN'T GET ANY BETTER THAN THAT!
WE COULD HAVE DEFEATED THEM PERMANENTLY AND WITHOUT ANYONE GETTING KILLED. THAT WOULD'VE BEEN BETTER.

YEAH, WHAT'S UP WITH LETTING THEM GO?
VICTORY IS NOT MEASURED IN GAINS AND LOSSES, BUSHWACKY.
YES IT IS.
WELL, I'M MORE OF AN EYE FOR AN EYE KIND OF GUY.
LOOK, WE WENT OVER THIS. OUR MISSION IS TO GET BACK OFF THIS PLANET WITH MINIMAL EFFECT.
WE MUSN'T HARM THE HUMANS BEYOND WHAT CAN'T BE AVOIDED.
THAT'S A STUPID RULE, WHO CAME UP WITH THAT?
YOU KNOW WHAT THAT SOUNDS LIKE TO ME... SOUNDS LIKE BIG RIG TALK.

WHAT'S THAT SUPPOSED TO MEAN?
YOU KNOW WHAT IT MEANS, RUSTY.
YEAH. YOU KNOW.
WHAT ARE YOU TALKING ABOUT?
EVER SINCE YOU JOINED THE RULING COUNCIL, YOU'VE BEEN SHOWING A DISTINCT AWESOMEBOT FLAVOR TO YOUR DECISIONS.
THAT'S RIDICULOUS. WHY WOULD I AUTOMATICALLY SIDE WITH THE AWESOME-BOTS?
C'MON, RUSTY, DROP THE CHARADE. YOU KNOW. YOU'RE ORANGE...
...BIG RIG IS ORANGE...

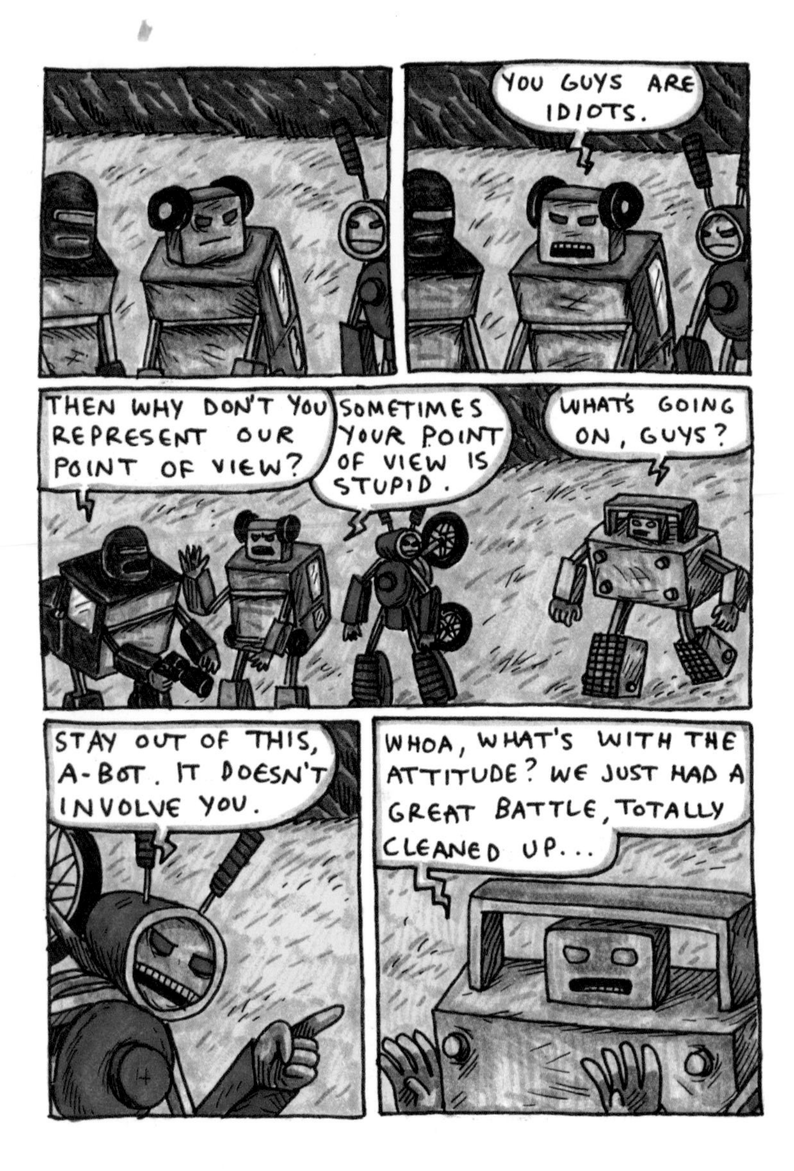
YOU GUYS ARE IDIOTS.
THEN WHY DON'T YOU REPRESENT OUR POINT OF VIEW?
SOMETIMES YOUR POINT OF VIEW IS STUPID.
WHAT'S GOING ON, GUYS?
STAY OUT OF THIS, A-BOT. IT DOESN'T INVOLVE YOU.
WHOA, WHAT'S WITH THE ATTITUDE? WE JUST HAD A GREAT BATTLE, TOTALLY CLEANED UP...

CLEANED UP? WE DIDN'T EVEN FINISH THEM OFF!
YEAH, FINISHING OFF IS AN INTEGRAL PART OF THE CLIMAX TO ANY BATTLE!
IF YOU DON'T KILL THEM ALL, THEY JUST COME BACK STRONGER!
AND BEAT YOU!
YOU'RE COMPLETELY WRONG.
IF I WAS WRONG, I WOULDN'T BE ARGUING WITH YOU!
LET'S ALL CALM DOWN, HERE. WE CAN AGREE TO DISAGREE.
DON'T TELL US WHAT TO DO!
WHAT WE NEED TO DO IS REFORM THE FANTASTICONS.
OF COURSE, WE'LL NEED A NEW LEADER...

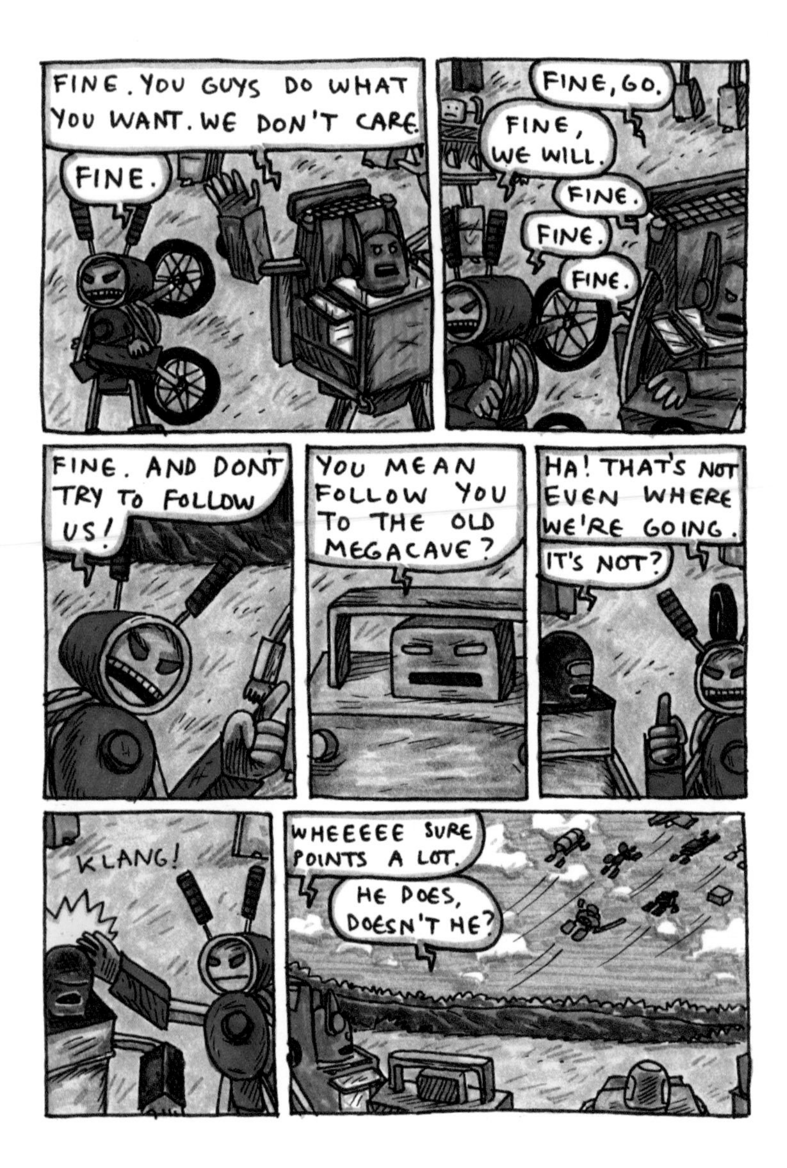
FINE. YOU GUYS DO WHAT YOU WANT. WE DON'T CARE.
FINE.
FINE, GO.
FINE, WE WILL.
FINE.
FINE.
FINE.
FINE. AND DON'T TRY TO FOLLOW US!
YOU MEAN FOLLOW YOU TO THE OLD MEGACAVE?
HA! THAT'S NOT EVEN WHERE WE'RE GOING.
IT'S NOT?
KLANG!
WHEEEEE SURE POINTS A LOT.
HE DOES, DOESN'T HE?

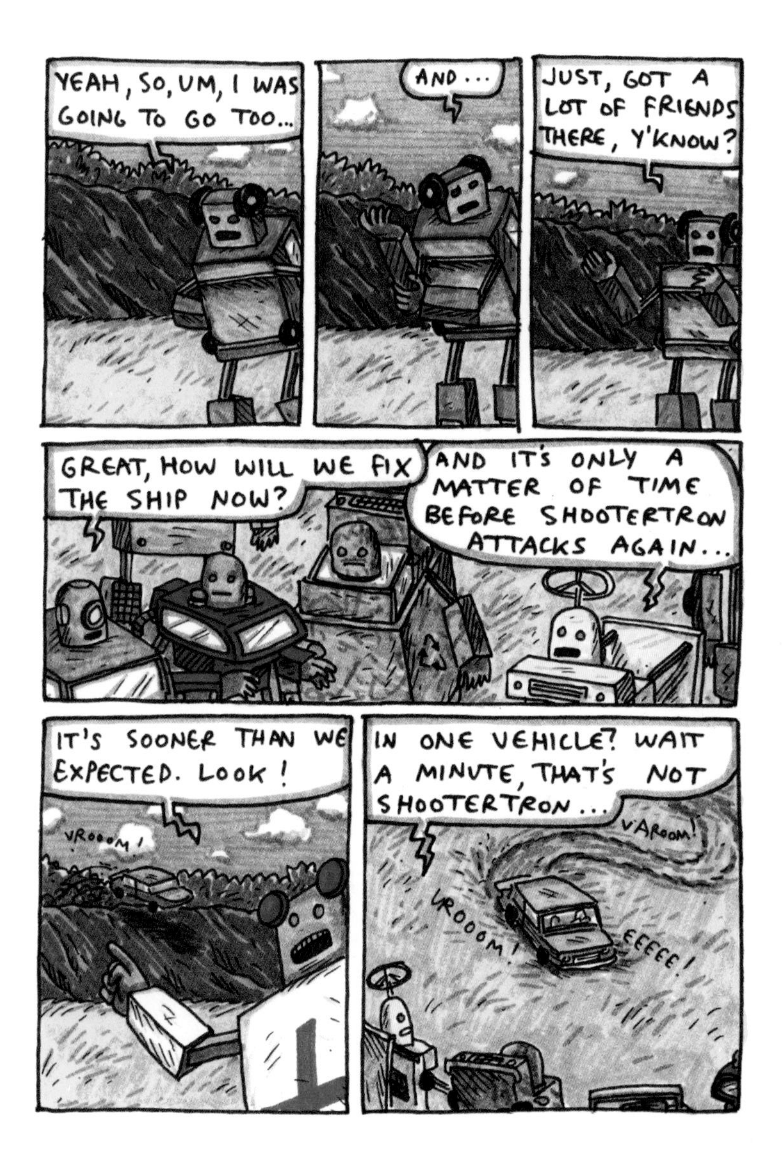
YEAH, SO, UM, I WAS GOING TO GO TOO...
AND...
JUST, GOT A LOT OF FRIENDS THERE, Y'KNOW?
GREAT, HOW WILL WE FIX THE SHIP NOW?
AND IT'S ONLY A MATTER OF TIME BEFORE SHOOTERTRON ATTACKS AGAIN...
IT'S SOONER THAN WE EXPECTED. LOOK!
VROOOM!
IN ONE VEHICLE? WAIT A MINUTE, THAT'S NOT SHOOTERTRON...
VAROOM!
VROOOM!
EEEEEE!

YOU'RE BACK!
IT'S TRUE! I KNEW IT!
JIMMY JR?
BALLS!
BIG RIG! HIGH FIVE!
YEAH!
IT'S COOL, NEVER MIND. IT'S SO GREAT TO SEE YOU ALL AGAIN!
IT'S GOOD TO SEE YOU TOO, JIMMY JR...
AND-MONKEYWRENCH?!
BUT YOU'RE DEAD*!!
WHAT?!
* SEE INCREDIBLE CHANGE-BOTS BOOK ONE. MONKEYWRENCH TOTALLY GOT KILLED! IT WAS VERY TRAUMATIC.

(FROM L TO R): JIMMY JR, MONKEYWRENCH,
BALLS. AT THE AWESOMEBASE.
MARCH 18, 2007

SO, IT'S LIKE OLD TIMES...
WOW, THE MEGACAVE LOOKS EXACTLY HOW WE LEFT IT.
I GUESS WE LEFT IT AS KIND OF A MESS.
STILL, IT FEELS LIKE SOMETHING'S MISSING WITHOUT SHOOTERTRON HERE.
PERHAPS NOT.
GASP!

SHOOTERTRON!
HOP
WHAT ARE YOU DOING?
IT'S AN EARTH GREETING OF BROTHERHOOD CALLED A HUG.
PLEASE DON'T.
I'M SORRY I STARTED SHOOTING AT EVERYONE BACK THERE. I DIDN'T SHOOT FOR A FEW YEARS, AND I JUST STARTED SHOOTING THINGS AGAIN, SO I STILL GET A LITTLE BIT WORKED UP...

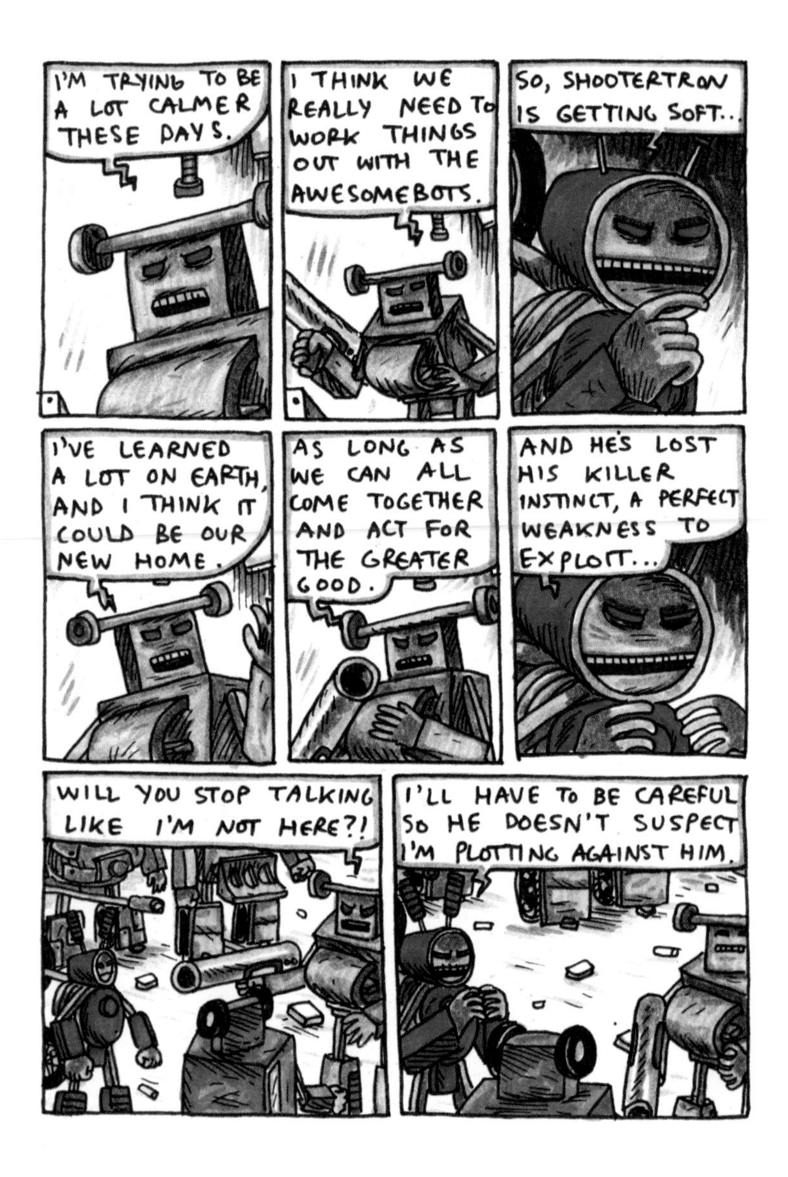
I'M TRYING TO BE A LOT CALMER THESE DAYS.
I THINK WE REALLY NEED TO WORK THINGS OUT WITH THE AWESOMEBOTS.
SO, SHOOTERTRON IS GETTING SOFT...
I'VE LEARNED A LOT ON EARTH, AND I THINK IT COULD BE OUR NEW HOME.
AS LONG AS WE CAN ALL COME TOGETHER AND ACT FOR THE GREATER GOOD.
AND HE'S LOST HIS KILLER INSTINCT, A PERFECT WEAKNESS TO EXPLOIT...
WILL YOU STOP TALKING LIKE I'M NOT HERE?!
I'LL HAVE TO BE CAREFUL SO HE DOESN'T SUSPECT I'M PLOTTING AGAINST HIM.

ANYWAY, I'VE GOT SOME NEW TECHNOLOGY FOR US. FIRST, I'LL FIT YOU ALL WITH THESE HYBRID PLUTONIUM REACTORS.
THERE. HOW DOES THAT FEEL?
UM, IT KIND OF HURTS. A LOT.
HM. MAYBE I PUT IT IN WRONG?
BECAUSE OF THE... ELECTRON SPIN, YOU KNOW? THEY SPIN RIGHT... OR LEFT?
WHAT ARE YOU TALKING ABOUT?
ELECTRON SPIN? IT'S LIKE... UH, I UNDERSTAND IT, I JUST DON'T KNOW HOW TO EXPLAIN IT...
THERE. BETTER?
YEAH, THAT'S GREAT!
LOOK HOW FAST I CAN INCREDIBLE CHANGE NOW!
INCREDIBLE CHANGE!
CHEE CHOO CHE CHEE CHOO CHOOK

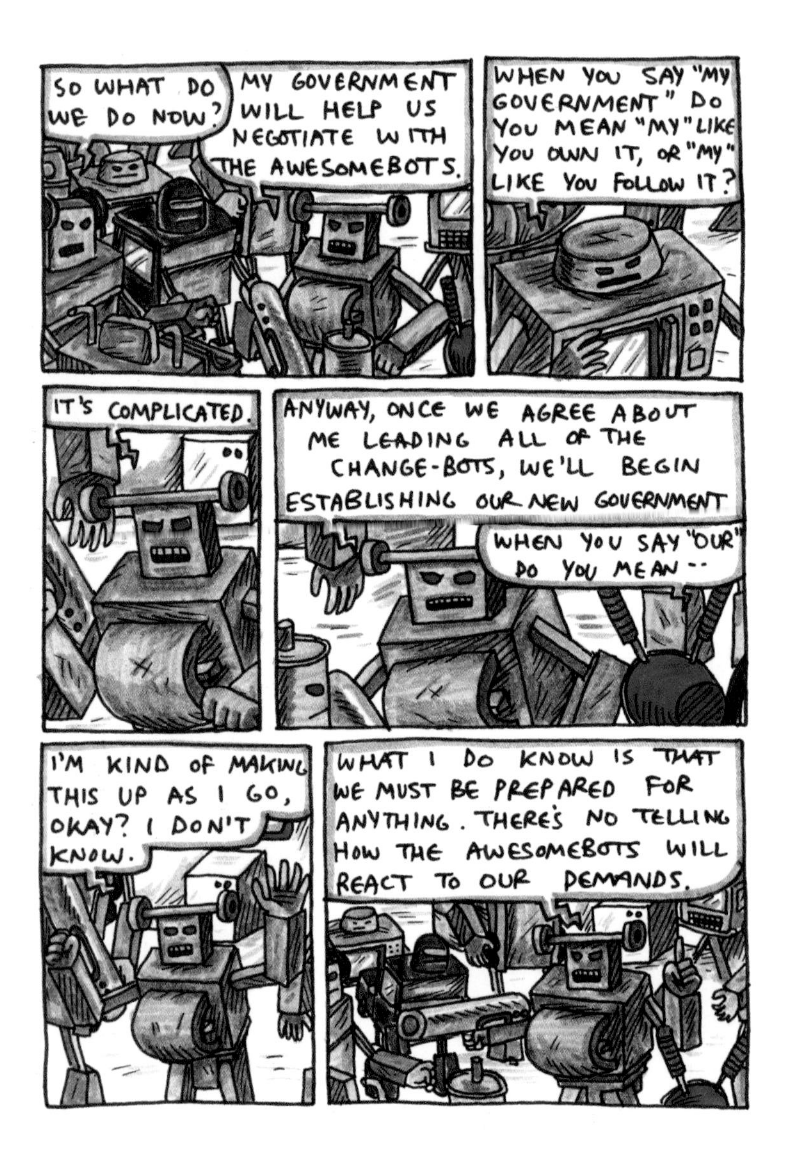
SO WHAT DO WE DO NOW?
MY GOVERNMENT WILL HELP US NEGOTIATE WITH THE AWESOMEBOTS.
WHEN YOU SAY "MY GOVERNMENT" DO YOU MEAN "MY" LIKE YOU OWN IT, OR "MY" LIKE YOU FOLLOW IT?
IT'S COMPLICATED.
ANYWAY, ONCE WE AGREE ABOUT ME LEADING ALL OF THE CHANGE-BOTS, WE'LL BEGIN ESTABLISHING OUR NEW GOVERNMENT
WHEN YOU SAY "OUR" DO YOU MEAN--
I'M KIND OF MAKING THIS UP AS I GO, OKAY? I DON'T KNOW.
WHAT I DO KNOW IS THAT WE MUST BE PREPARED FOR ANYTHING. THERE'S NO TELLING HOW THE AWESOMEBOTS WILL REACT TO OUR DEMANDS.

MEANWHILE!
DEAD?! WHAT ARE YOU TALKING ABOUT?
YOU DIED.
HUH?
SAY, BIG RIG, CAN I TALK TO YOU A MINUTE?
LOOK, BOTH OF OUR CONTINUITY RECORDINGS SAY MONKEYWRENCH DIED, RIGHT?
YEAH.
THAT CAN MEAN ONLY ONE THING.
OH NO.
YEP. TIME TRAVELERS.
OH MAN, I DON'T EVEN WANT TO THINK ABOUT IT...
GUYS RUNNING AROUND, SCREWING UP CONTINUITY...
I KNOW, I KNOW.
I THINK WE JUST NEED TO IGNORE IT. ACT NORMAL.
OKAY, OKAY, YEAH. LET'S PLAY IT COOL.

MONKEYWRENCH! JIMMY JR! SO GOOD TO SEE YOU BOTH AGAIN!
YOU BOTH LOOK LIKE YOU'VE... GROWN UP...
THANKS!
IT'S GOOD TO SEE ALL OF YOU TOO, BUT WHAT BRINGS YOU BACK TO EARTH?
IT'S A LONG STORY.
OKAY.
REALLY, REALLY, REALLY LONG.
OKAY.

ANYWAY, LET'S SAY HELLO TO SOME OF THE OTHERS...
HOSER!
I GOT A REDESIGN!
AND STINKY!
LOOK, I'VE CONVERTED INTO A RECYCLING TRUCK.
AND--WHO ARE YOU?
IT'S ME!
SHADOW XGX-9!
UM, WHO?
DON'T YOU REMEMBER?
WE FOUGHT THE FANTASTICONS TOGETHER?
ER...

HONKYTONK AND SIREN! YOU'RE ALIVE?
YES, IVY MANAGED TO REPAIR US.
BUT IT'S UP TO US TO REPAIR OUR RELATIONSHIP.
SIREN JUST NEEDS SOME T.L.C.
AWWWW
TOTAL LOGISTICAL CONTROL.
OH.
SHE NEEDS SOMEONE TO KEEP HER IN LINE.
THAT DOESN'T SOUND HEALTHY...
DON'T TRY TO UNDERSTAND OUR LOVE.
HOW ABOUT YOU, JIMMY JR., HAVE YOU FOUND AN EARTH WOMAN COMPANION SINCE WE LEFT?
YEAH, LET ME SHOW YOU A PICTURE!
HM, YES. I'M SURE SHE'S VERY ATTRACTIVE BY HUMAN STANDARDS

SO EJECT, WHAT SHOULD OUR PLAN BE?
I STILL GET TO BE ON THE COUNCIL? AW, THANKS, BIG RIG!
I THINK OUR PLAN SHOULD BE TO ESTABLISH BASE DEFENSES WHILE WE ASSESS THE DAMAGE TO OUR SPACECRAFT.
IF WE JUST CARVE OUT OUR OWN LITTLE TERRITORY HERE, I'M SURE THE HUMANS WON'T MIND, AND PERHAPS THE FANTASTICONS WILL LET US BE.
HEY WAIT, IT'S MICROWAVE!
HEY GUYS, I'M JUST HERE TO..
HE'S SPYING!
GET HIM!
NO, WAIT, I JUST DIDN'T WANT TO INTERRUPT---
GRAB HIM!
HEY, LET GO!

WE'LL MAKE YOU TALK!
WHAT?! NO, I'LL TALK! I CAME TO TALK!
WHAT IS THAT? IS THAT TINFOIL? WHAT ARE YOU DOING WITH THAT TINFOIL? NOOOOOO!
BEEP BEEP
AIEEEEEEEE!
BZZZ
MAYBE WE SHOULD ACTUALLY GIVE HIM A CHANCE TO TALK?
AIEEEEE!
BZZZZZTTTTT
OH, YEAH.
OKAY.
BEEP
AGGHH! WHAT'S WRONG WITH YOU GUYS?! I'M JUST THE MESSENGER!
KOFF KOFF
OKAY, FANTASTICON. TALK.
SHOOTERTRON WANTS TO SET UP AN ARBITRATION HEARING.

I'M TRANSMITTING THE COORDINATES AND TIME TO YOU NOW.
BEEP BEEP BO BEEP
AND IF YOU DON'T SHOW UP, I WILL DESTROY YOU ALL!
WHAT?!
SHOOTERTRON WILL DESTROY YOU ALL, I MEAN.
NOT ME. I WAS JUST SAYING WHAT HE SAID.
SOUPY! POPPER! LET'S GO!
INCREDIBLE CHANGE!
CHEE CHOO CHEE
CHOO CHEE
CHOOK CHOO
CHEE CHU
INCREDIBLE CHANGE!
CHEE CHOO CHEE
CHEE
CHEE CHOOK CHOO
CHEE
WE'LL JUST WALK BACK.

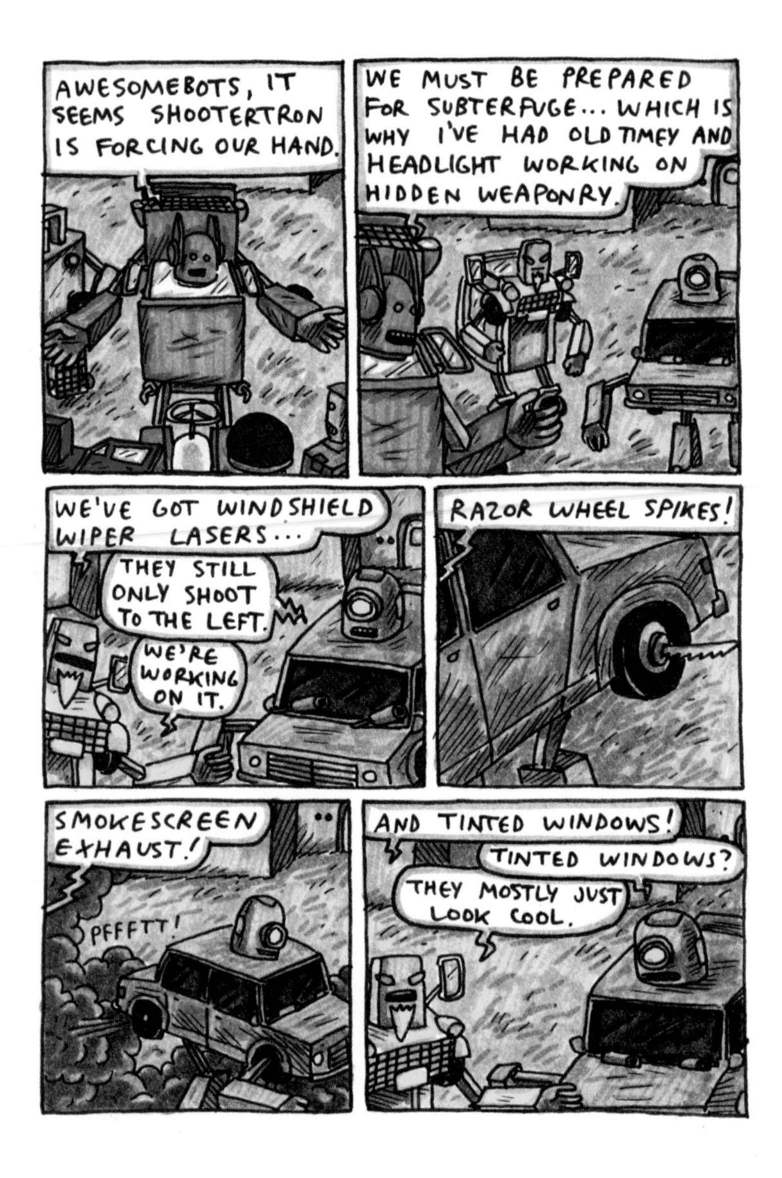
AWESOMEBOTS, IT SEEMS SHOOTERTRON IS FORCING OUR HAND.
WE MUST BE PREPARED FOR SUBTERFUGE... WHICH IS WHY I'VE HAD OLD TIMEY AND HEADLIGHT WORKING ON HIDDEN WEAPONRY.
WE'VE GOT WINDSHIELD WIPER LASERS...
THEY STILL ONLY SHOOT TO THE LEFT.
WE'RE WORKING ON IT.
RAZOR WHEEL SPIKES!
SMOKESCREEN EXHAUST!
PFFFTT!
AND TINTED WINDOWS!
TINTED WINDOWS?
THEY MOSTLY JUST LOOK COOL.

BIG RIG, MAYBE WE SHOULD GO WITH YOU, SO YOU HAVE SOME HUMANS ALONG.
NO, THAT'S OKAY. IT'S TOO DANGEROUS.
BUT WE COULD HELP WITH YOUR IMAGE, MAKE YOU SEEM LESS ALIEN?
I'M AFRAID YOU MIGHT BE A DISTRACTION.
WE COULD HELP YOU INTERPRET THE HUMAN SUBTLETIES INVOLVED.
NO, I'M SURE WE'LL MOSTLY BE DEALING WITH THE FANTASTICONS.
WE COULD BE YOUR HUMAN SHIELDS.
OKAY, YOU CAN COME WITH US.
YAY!

THE NEXT DAY!
SHOOTERTRON! THE AWESOMEBOTS ARE APPROACHING!
OH, IT LOOKS LIKE THEY'RE ALL COMING...
YEAH, IS THAT BAD?
NO.
I DIDN'T THINK THEY'D ALL COME.
IF I HAD KNOWN THAT, I WOULD'VE SENT SOME GUYS TO ATTACK THEIR BASE OR SOMETHING.
OKAY, EVERYBODY STAY COOL.

INCREDIBLE CHANGE!
CHEE CHOO CHEE
CHOO CHOOK CHEE CHOO
WE'RE HERE, SHOOTERTRON. NOW, WHAT DO YOU WANT?
FIRST, LET ME INTRODUCE OUR TEAM OF LAWYERS.
YOU BROUGHT LAWYERS?
GREG MATHEWS
MARILYN WAGNER
JUDITH WINTERS
JOSEPH BROWN
AND MY LITERARY AGENT, GERALD MARKS.
YOU HAVE A LITERARY AGENT?

HEY, WHY ARE YOU HOLDING YOUR HANDS BEHIND YOUR BACK? WHAT DO YOU HAVE?
DON'T BE PARANOID, I DON'T HAVE ANYTHING.
WELL, EXCEPT THESE PAPERS.
THE FIRST SIGN OF A CONSPIRACY IS PEOPLE CALLING YOU PARANOID.
WELL, GENTLEMEN, LET'S GET THIS OVER WITH SHALL WE?
WE JUST NEED YOU EACH TO SIGN THESE PAPERS. I'VE MARKED ALL THE PLACES YOU NEED TO PUT YOUR SIGNATURES.
THAT'S IT? OKAY.
WAIT, WAIT WAIT... WHAT DO THESE PAPERS SAY?
JUST THAT SHOOTERTRON WILL BE YOUR SOLE LEADER FOREVER AND EVER.
DO YOU NEED PENS?

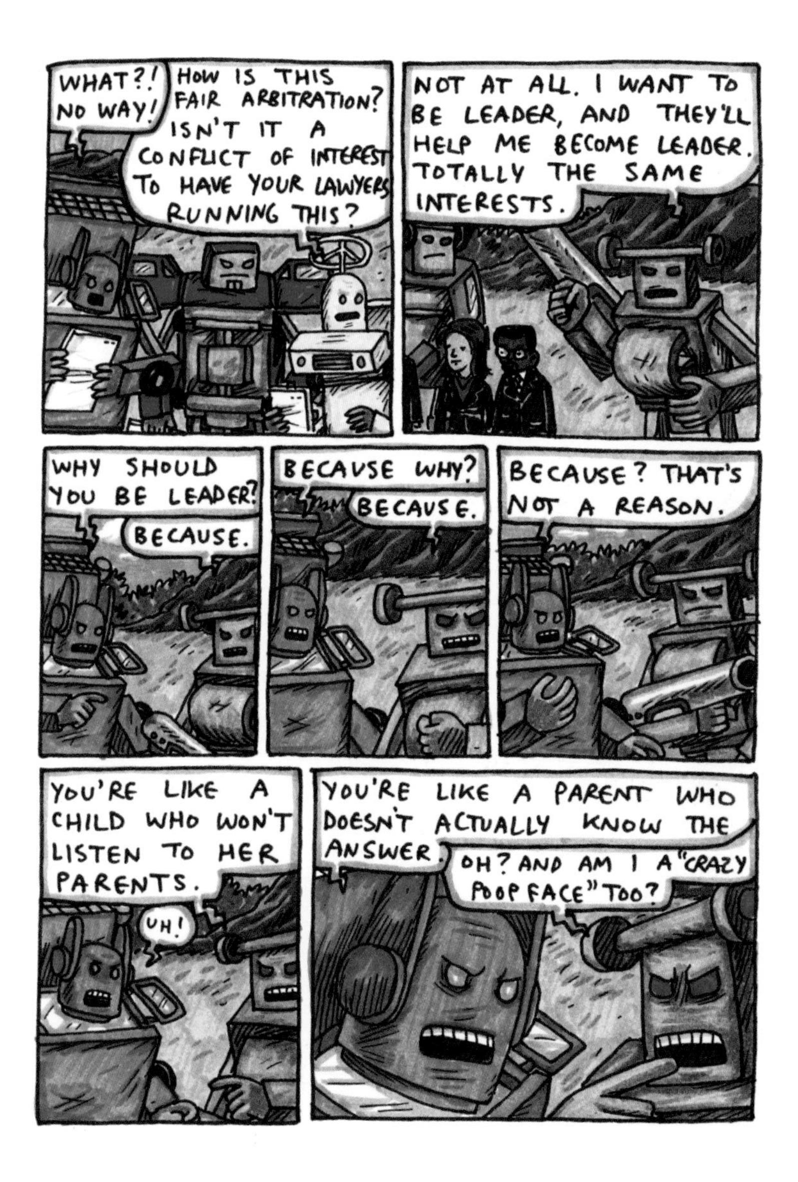
WHAT?! NO WAY!
HOW IS THIS FAIR ARBITRATION? ISN'T IT A CONFLICT OF INTEREST TO HAVE YOUR LAWYERS RUNNING THIS?
NOT AT ALL. I WANT TO BE LEADER, AND THEY'LL HELP ME BECOME LEADER. TOTALLY THE SAME INTERESTS.
WHY SHOULD YOU BE LEADER?
BECAUSE.
BECAUSE WHY?
BECAUSE.
BECAUSE? THAT'S NOT A REASON.
YOU'RE LIKE A CHILD WHO WON'T LISTEN TO HER PARENTS.
UH!
YOU'RE LIKE A PARENT WHO DOESN'T ACTUALLY KNOW THE ANSWER.
OH? AND AM I A "CRAZY POOP FACE" TOO?

FELLOW CHANGEBOTS, ALLOW ME TO SPEAK.
INCREDIBLE CHANGE!
CHEE CHOO CHEE CHOO
THE CONFLICT BETWEEN AWESOMEBOTS AND FANTASTICONS HAS RAGED FOR MANY YEARS.
EVEN IN TIMES OF PEACE, WE HAVE TROUBLE RECONCILING OUR DIFFERENCES.
INCREDIBLE CHANGE!
CHEE CHOOK CHEE CHU
DESPITE OUR ABILITY TO CHANGE OUR PHYSICAL FORMS...

... WE APPEAR UNABLE TO CHANGE ON THE INSIDE.
INCREDIBLE CHANGE!
CHEE CHOOK CHOO CHEE CHOO
PERHAPS WE DO NOT EVEN DESERVE TO BE CALLED CHANGE-BOTS.
I BELIEVE THAT WE - WE --
INCREDIBLE CHANGE!
CHEE CHOO CHEE CHOOK
WILL YOU STOP THAT?!
SORRY. I'M BORED.

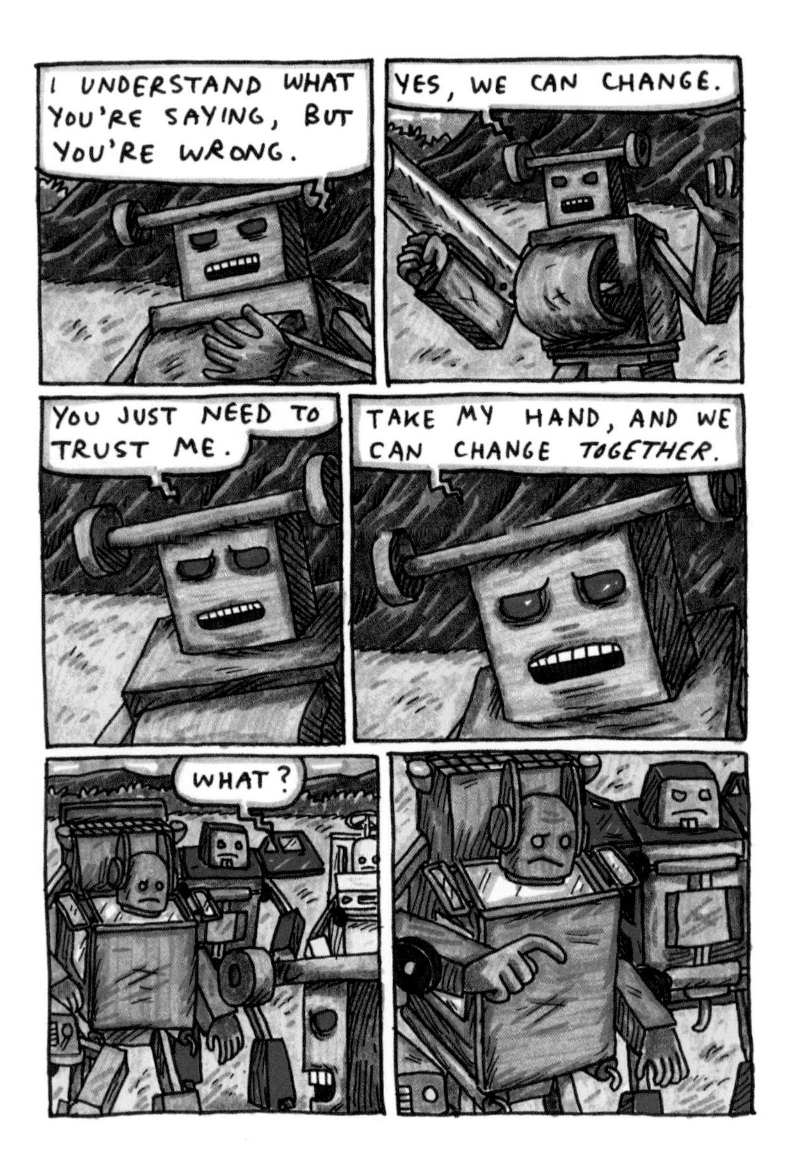
I UNDERSTAND WHAT YOU'RE SAYING, BUT YOU'RE WRONG.
YES, WE CAN CHANGE.
YOU JUST NEED TO TRUST ME.
TAKE MY HAND, AND WE CAN CHANGE *TOGETHER*.
WHAT?

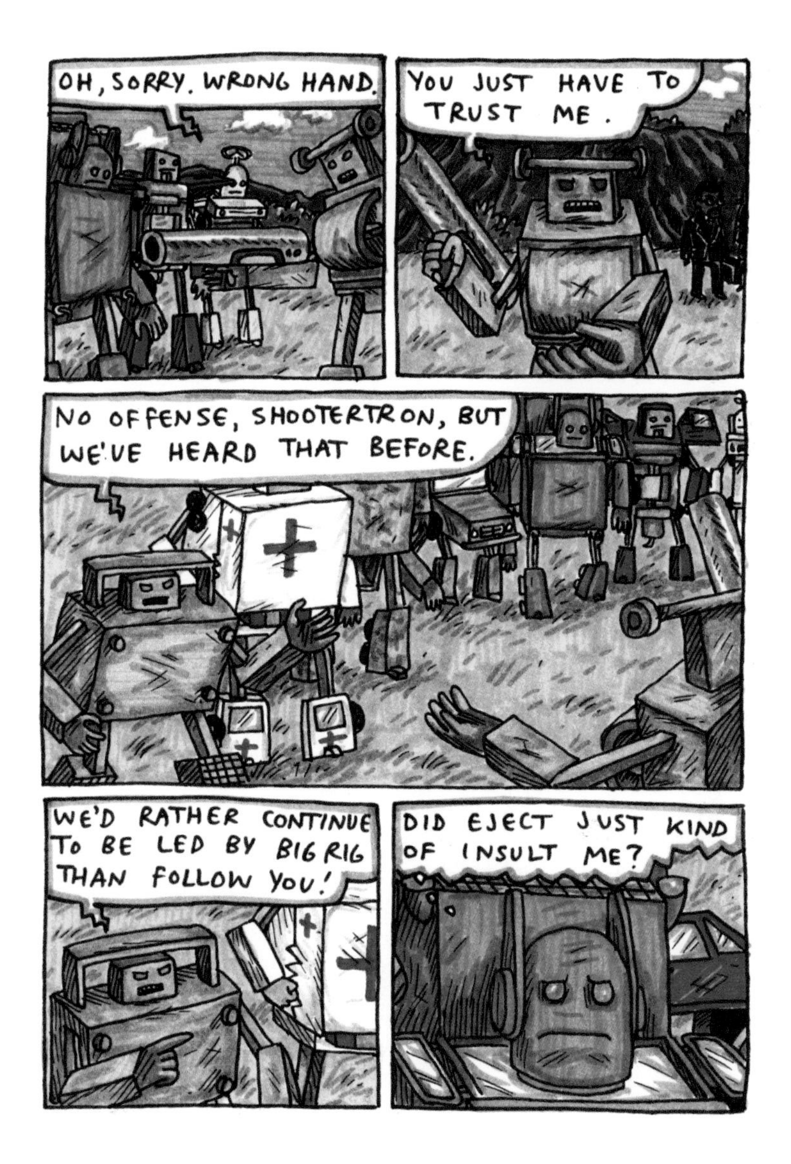
OH, SORRY. WRONG HAND.
YOU JUST HAVE TO TRUST ME.
NO OFFENSE, SHOOTERTRON, BUT WE'VE HEARD THAT BEFORE.
WE'D RATHER CONTINUE TO BE LED BY BIG RIG THAN FOLLOW YOU!
DID EJECT JUST KIND OF INSULT ME?

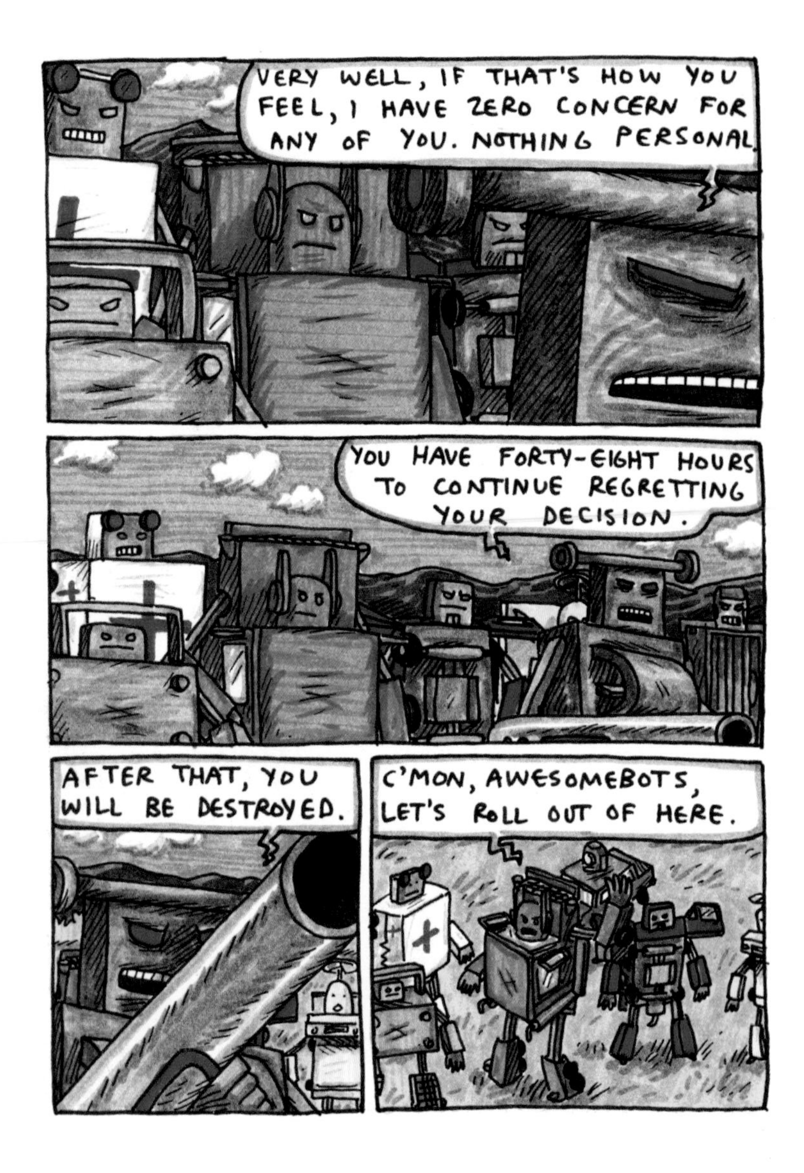
VERY WELL, IF THAT'S HOW YOU FEEL, I HAVE ZERO CONCERN FOR ANY OF YOU. NOTHING PERSONAL.
YOU HAVE FORTY-EIGHT HOURS TO CONTINUE REGRETTING YOUR DECISION.
AFTER THAT, YOU WILL BE DESTROYED.
C'MON, AWESOMEBOTS, LET'S ROLL OUT OF HERE.

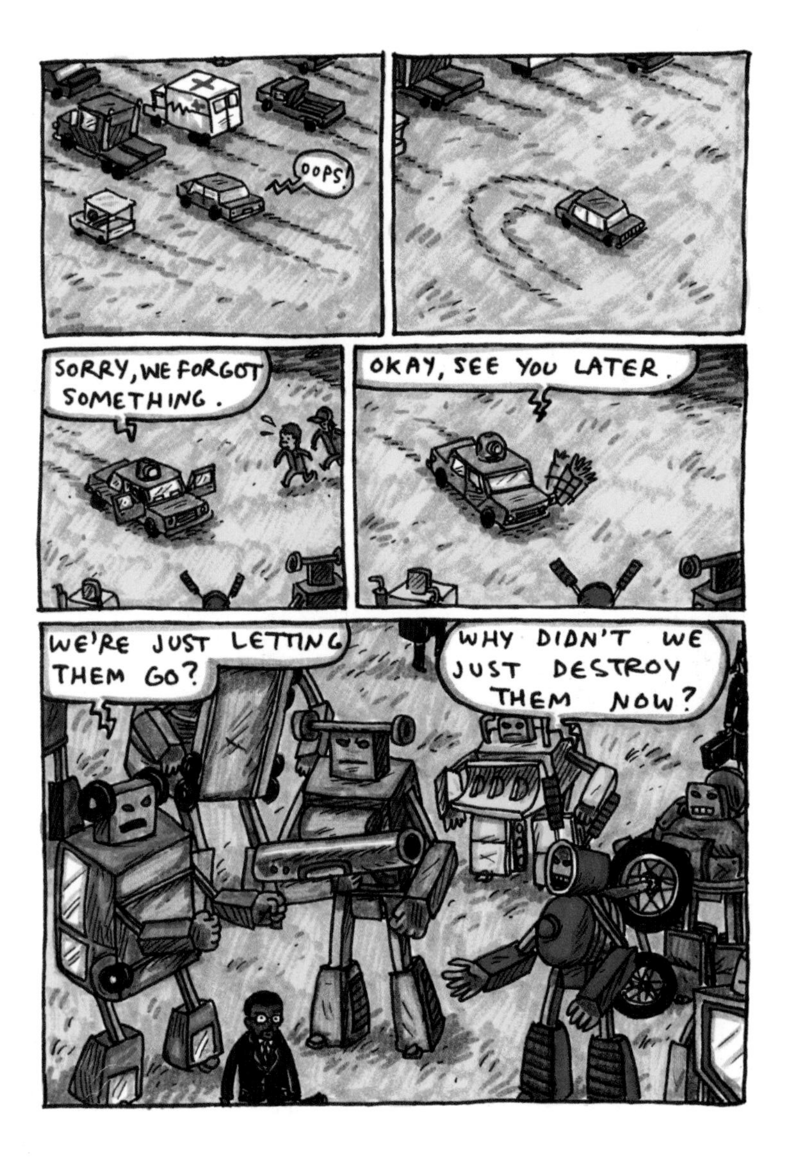
OOPS!
SORRY, WE FORGOT SOMETHING.
OKAY, SEE YOU LATER.
WE'RE JUST LETTING THEM GO?
WHY DIDN'T WE JUST DESTROY THEM NOW?

IT'S PART OF MY NEW PHILOSOPHY. WE'LL LET THEM THINK THINGS OVER, THEN TALK TO THEM AGAIN.
VIOLENCE DOESN'T SOLVE ANYTHING, BUT TALKING DOES.
DIDN'T WE JUST SPEND THE WHOLE DAY TALKING WITHOUT SOLVING ANYTHING?
YOU DIDN'T LET ME FINISH.
VIOLENCE DOESN'T SOLVE ANYTHING...
BUT TALKING WITH GUNS DOES!
I LIKE GUNS!

BOOM!

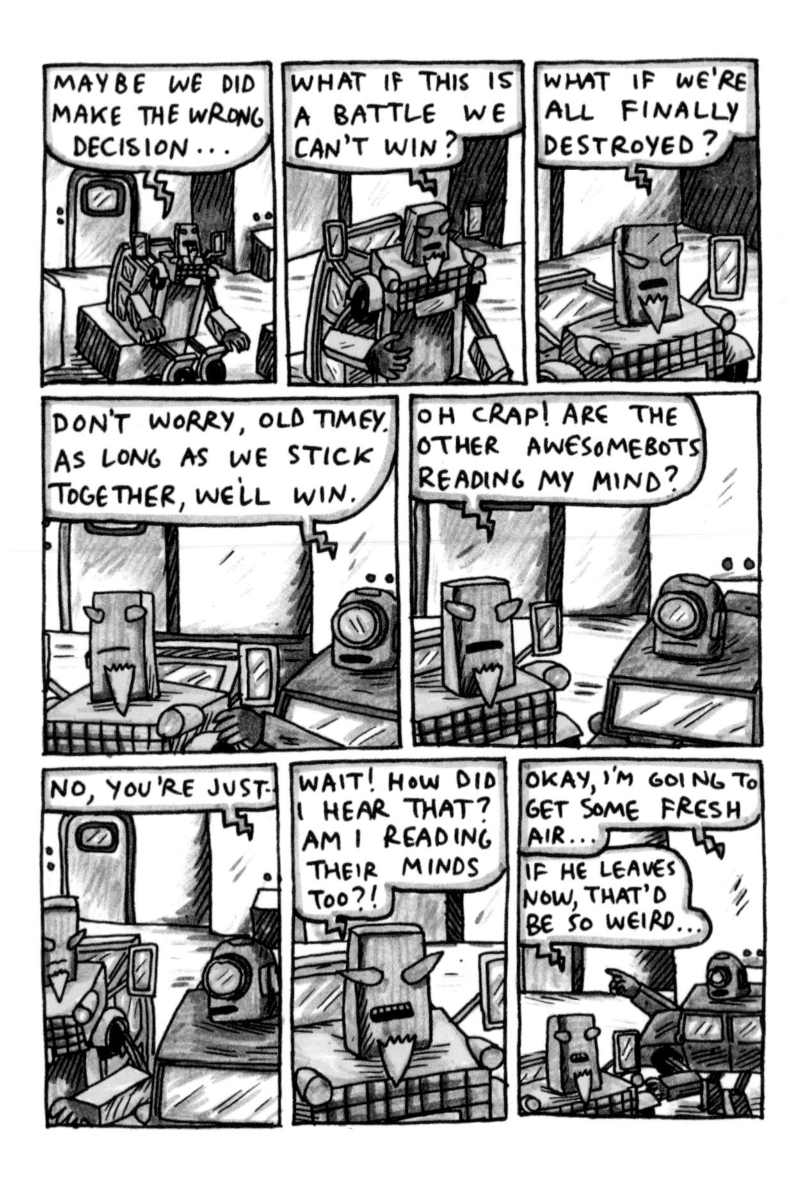
MAYBE WE DID MAKE THE WRONG DECISION...
WHAT IF THIS IS A BATTLE WE CAN'T WIN?
WHAT IF WE'RE ALL FINALLY DESTROYED?
DON'T WORRY, OLD TIMEY. AS LONG AS WE STICK TOGETHER, WE'LL WIN.
OH CRAP! ARE THE OTHER AWESOMEBOTS READING MY MIND?
NO, YOU'RE JUST-
WAIT! HOW DID I HEAR THAT? AM I READING THEIR MINDS TOO?!
OKAY, I'M GOING TO GET SOME FRESH AIR...
IF HE LEAVES NOW, THAT'D BE SO WEIRD...

WHAT NOW, BIG RIG?
JIMMY JR. AND BALLS ARE USING LAPTOPOR TO TRY AND HACK INTO THE FANTASTICON DATABASE.
ANY LUCK?
TAK TAK TAK TAK TAK TAK
SHOOT... ACCORDING TO THIS, THEY PRINTED ALL THEIR FILES OUT AS HARD COPIES.
GIGGLE
TAK TAK TAK
SO WE'LL NEED TO FIND THE HARD COPIES?
NO, AFTER THEY PRINTED IT ALL OUT, THEY SHREDDED IT ALL.
WE CAN ONLY GUESS WHAT THE FANTASTICONS ARE PLANNING.
NO MATTER. WE DON'T NEED TO KNOW THEIR PLANS. WE JUST NEED AN INSPIRING SPEECH.

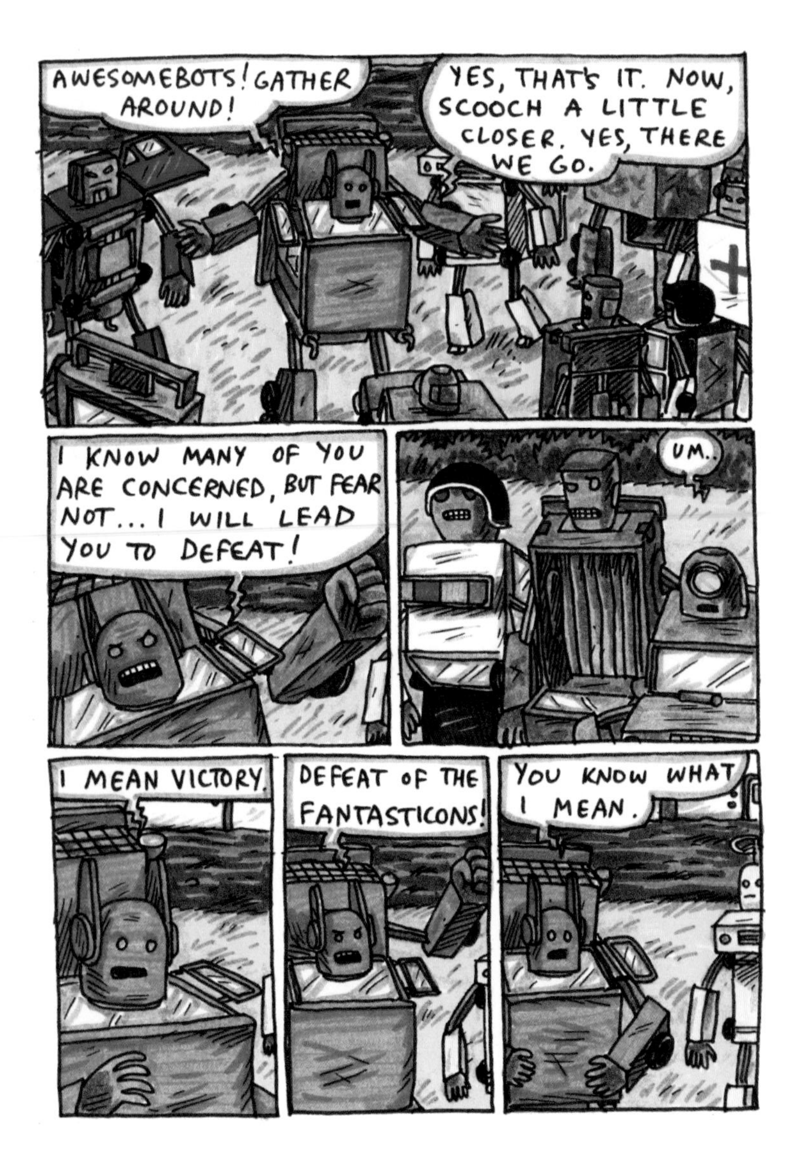
AWESOMEBOTS! GATHER AROUND!
YES, THAT'S IT. NOW, SCOOCH A LITTLE CLOSER. YES, THERE WE GO.
I KNOW MANY OF YOU ARE CONCERNED, BUT FEAR NOT... I WILL LEAD YOU TO DEFEAT!
UM..
I MEAN VICTORY.
DEFEAT OF THE FANTASTICONS!
YOU KNOW WHAT I MEAN.

WAIT, WHAT'S THAT? THE FANTASTICONS!
HOW DID THEY KNOW WE'D BE UNPREPARED?
JIMMY JR. UPDATED HIS SPACEBOOK STATUS TO "JUST HANGING OUT WITH MY MANBALLS :)"
SORRY.
HE ALSO DOWNLOADED SOME VIDEOS.
NO, I DIDN'T.
YES, WATCH, I'LL SHOW YOU.
I DIDN'T DOWNLOAD THOSE.
KLANG KLANG KLANG KLANG KLANG

AWESOMEBOTS! WE HAVE YOU SURROUNDED... SURRENDER, OR BE DESTROYED!
YOU DON'T HAVE US SURROUNDED, WE JUST MANAGED TO INFILTRATE THE CENTER OF YOUR FORCES!
HIGH FIVE
TENSION

WAIT! HOW CAN YOU DO THIS?
JUST DAYS AGO WE WERE FRIENDS
WHAT IS TIME TO A ROBOT?
WELL, WHAT IS A ROBOT... TO TIME?
HUH?
WHAT IS A ROBOT TO TIME?
HUH?
WE DON'T GET IT.
IT'S LIKE...
TIME IS... UM...
BEW! BEW!

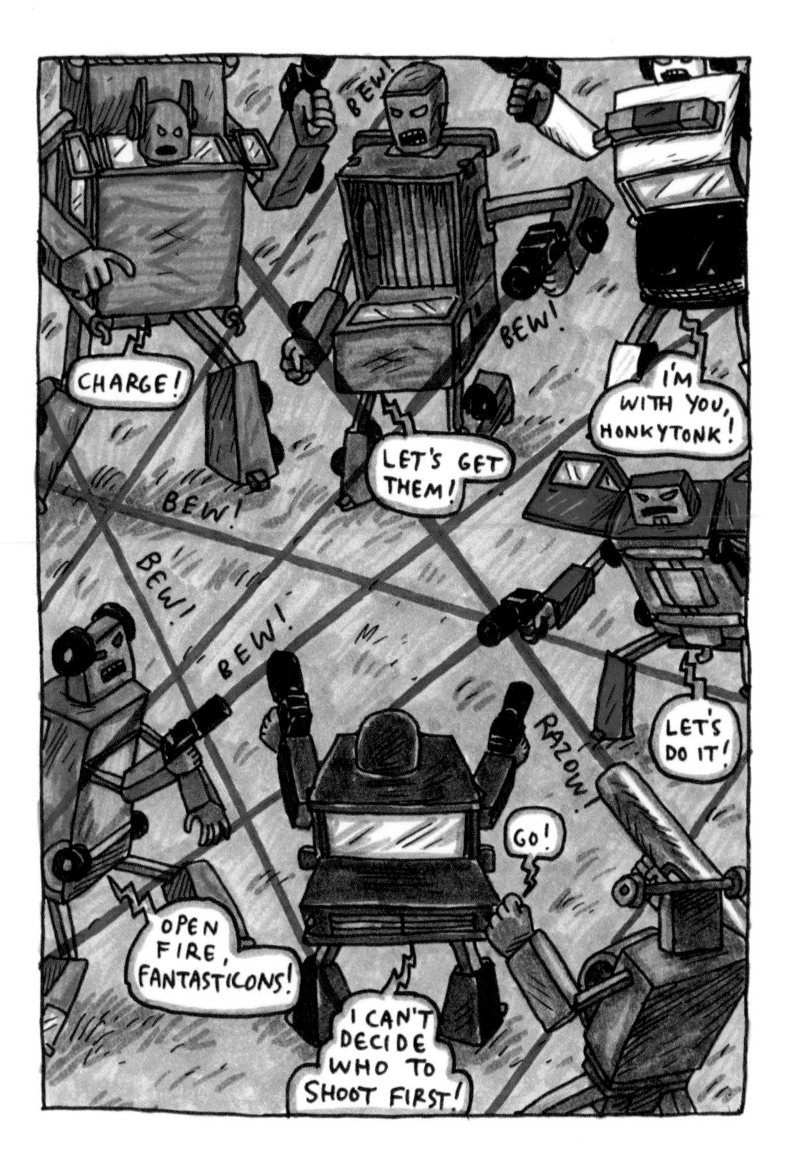
BEW!
CHARGE!
BEW!
LET'S GET THEM!
I'M WITH YOU, HONKYTONK!
BEW!
BEW!
BEW!
LET'S DO IT!
RAZOW!
GO!
OPEN FIRE, FANTASTICONS!
I CAN'T DECIDE WHO TO SHOOT FIRST!

REMEMBER, STINKY, NO ONE-LINERS!
DON'T WORRY, I'M NOT GOING TO REUSE ANY OLD JOKES.
TIME TO REDUCE YOUR FIGHTING CAPACITY!
RAGGHH!
AIEEEEE!
BEWP
YOU'RE KIND OF SCARING ME, MAN.
HELP ME STUFF HIM IN HERE, I'VE GOT TO RECYCLE HIM.
STOP IT!

WAIT, WHO ARE YOU?
I'M REJECTOR!
BEW!
BEW!
HEY, YOU CAN'T RIP OFF MY NAME!
WHATEVER, MY NAME IS TOTALLY DIFFERENT. PLUS, CAN YOU EVEN DO ANYTHING SIMILAR TO THIS?
BEEP
AUGGHH!
SHHPP
OH NO, TAPEY! I'M SO SORRY!

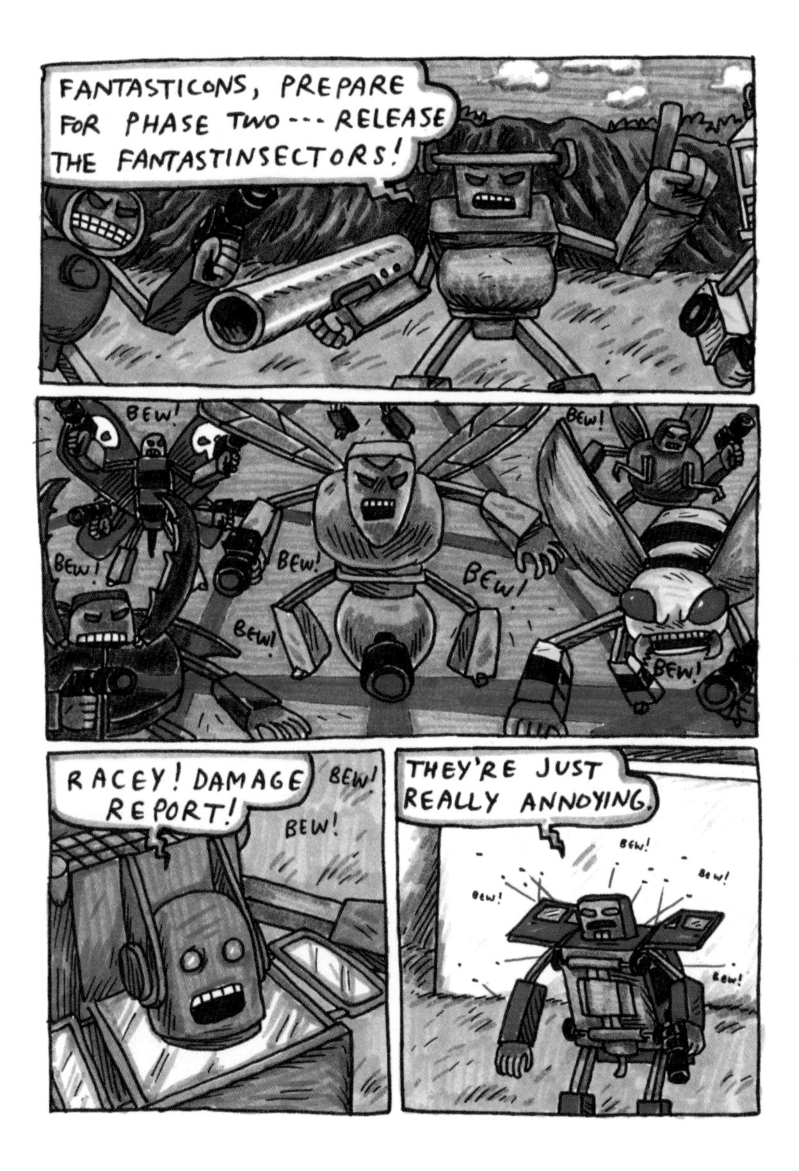
FANTASTICONS, PREPARE FOR PHASE TWO --- RELEASE THE FANTASTINSECTORS!
BEW!
BEW!
BEW!
BEW!
BEW!
BEW!
BEW!
RACEY! DAMAGE REPORT!
BEW!
BEW!
THEY'RE JUST REALLY ANNOYING.
BEW!
BEW!
BEW!
BEW!

AWESOMEBOTS, IT'S TIME TO RELEASE OUR SECRET WEAPONS--- SEND OUT THE AWESOMESAURUSES!
CHANGE-BOTS SHAPED LIKE EARTH DINOSAURS!
WHERE DID YOU GET THEM? BURIED DEEP UNDERGROUND?
BEW!
BEW!
BEW!
WE JUST MADE THEM.
WE THOUGHT THEY'D LOOK SWEET.
YEAH, THEY DO LOOK PRETTY SWAGGGHHH!
CRUNCH

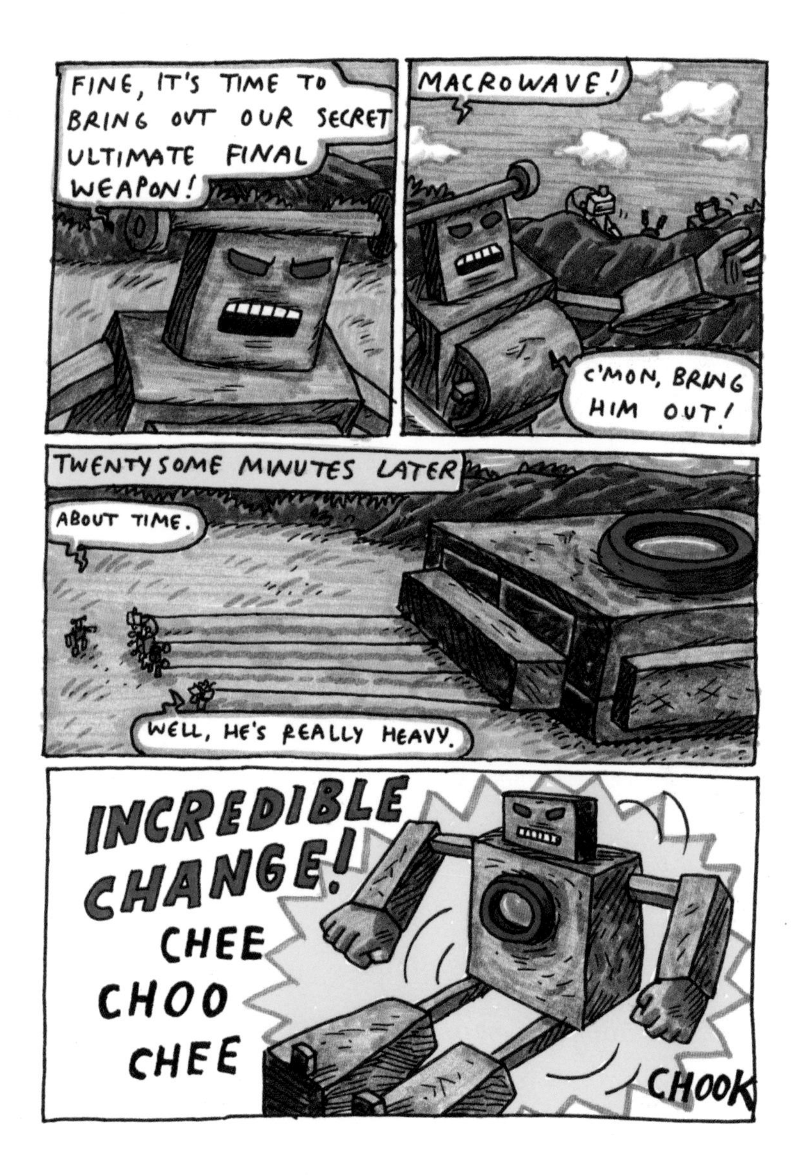
FINE, IT'S TIME TO BRING OUT OUR SECRET ULTIMATE FINAL WEAPON!
MACROWAVE!
C'MON, BRING HIM OUT!
TWENTYSOME MINUTES LATER
ABOUT TIME.
WELL, HE'S REALLY HEAVY.
INCREDIBLE CHANGE!
CHEE
CHOO
CHEE
CHOOK

MACROWAVE, ATTACK!
YEAH, THIS BATTLE'S TOTALLY OVER.
GET COVER!
AWESOMEBOTS! DON'T GIVE UP!
HE'S TOO BIG TO EXIST!
TEAMWORK, GUYS, TEAMWORK.
DADDY?
WHICH WAY DO WE RUN?

OUR WEAPONS SEEM TO HAVE NO EFFECT!
WAIT, LET'S TRY SHOOTING THE OTHER SIDE.
OVER HERE, GUYS!
BEW! BEW!
BEW!
BEW!
HEY, WAIT UP
IT'S WORKING!
BEW!
BEW!
BEW! BEW!
BEW!
BEW!
BEW!
BOOM!
YAYYY!
WE DID IT!

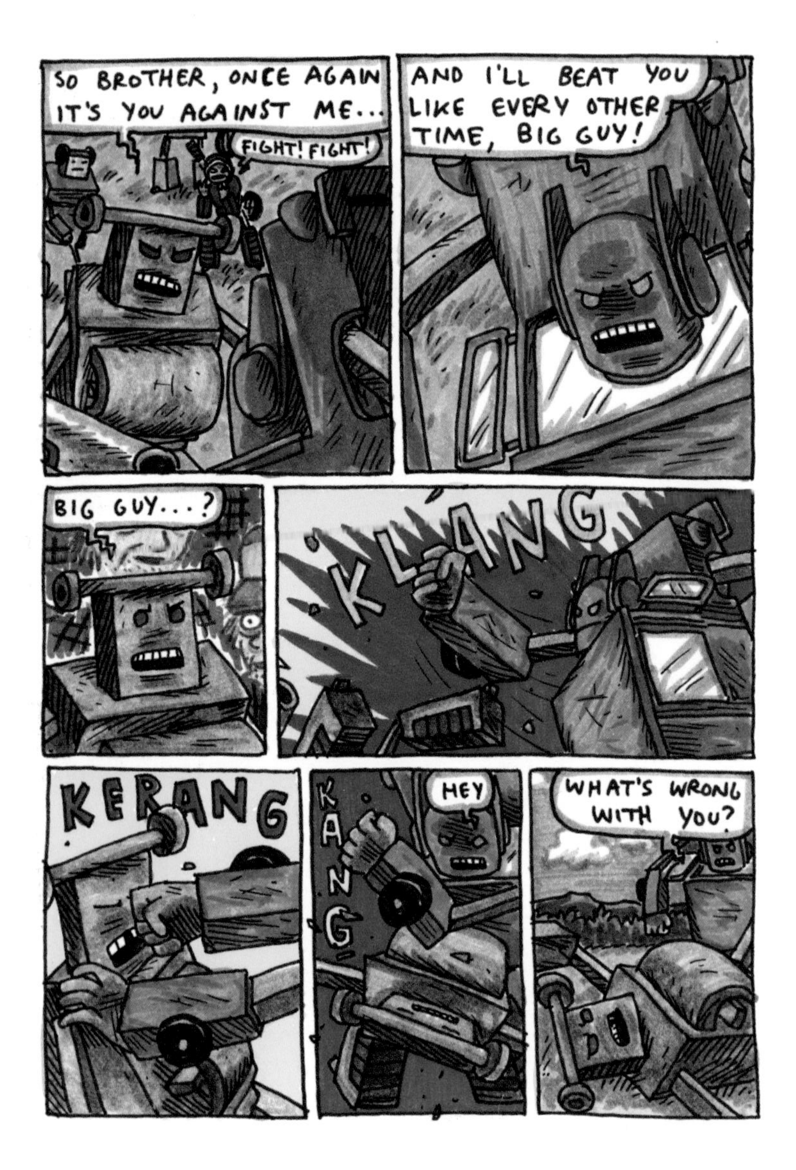
SO BROTHER, ONCE AGAIN IT'S YOU AGAINST ME...
FIGHT! FIGHT!
AND I'LL BEAT YOU LIKE EVERY OTHER TIME, BIG GUY!
BIG GUY...?
KLANG
KERANG
KANG
HEY
WHAT'S WRONG WITH YOU?

UH...
KICK
OKAY, THIS IS A LITTLE WEIRD.
KICK
KICK
KINCK
KICK
HEY!
POKE
POKE
POKE
YEAH, I'M TOTALLY WEIRDED OUT NOW.

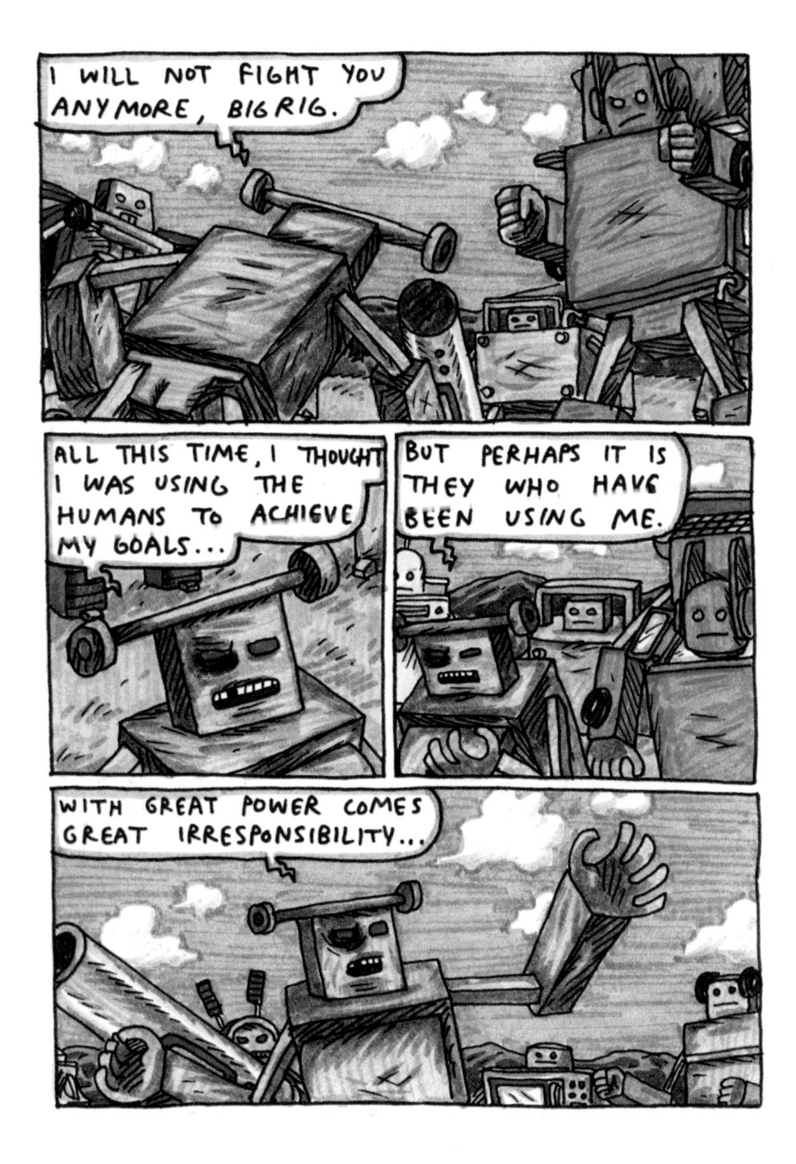
I WILL NOT FIGHT YOU ANYMORE, BIG RIG.
ALL THIS TIME, I THOUGHT I WAS USING THE HUMANS TO ACHIEVE MY GOALS...
BUT PERHAPS IT IS THEY WHO HAVE BEEN USING ME.
WITH GREAT POWER COMES GREAT IRRESPONSIBILITY...

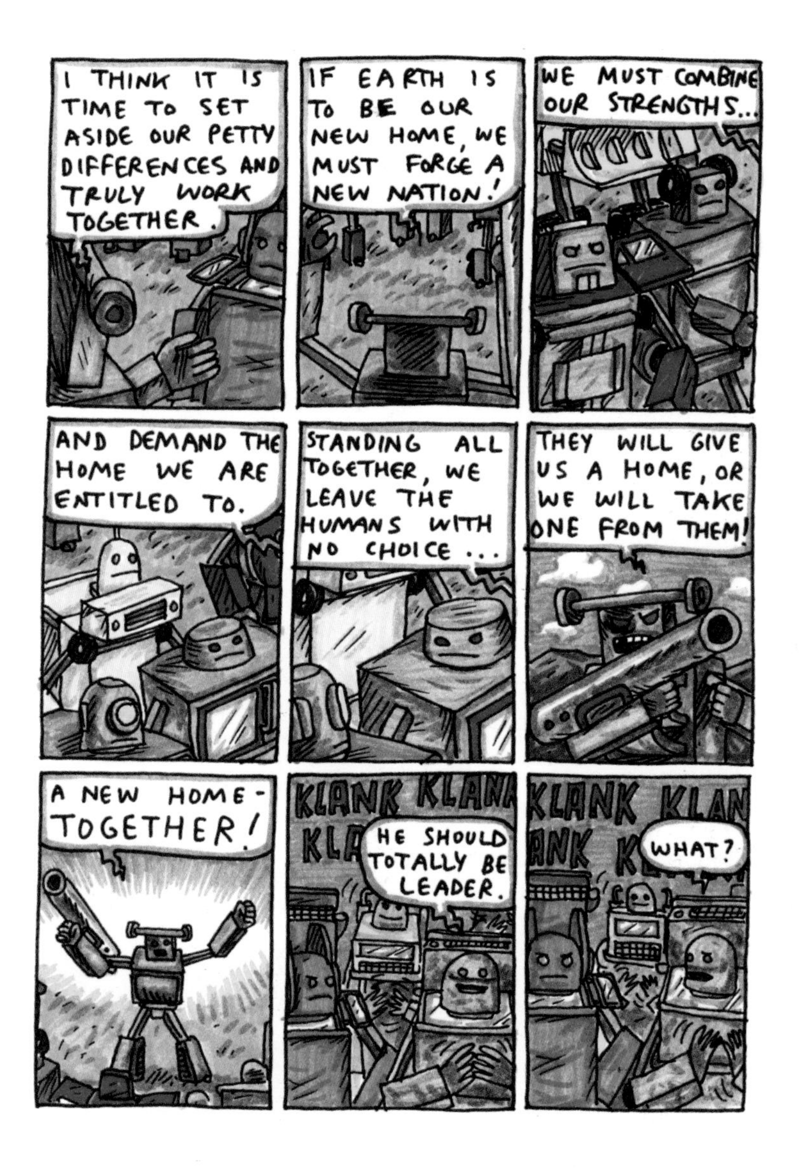
I THINK IT IS TIME TO SET ASIDE OUR PETTY DIFFERENCES AND TRULY WORK TOGETHER.
IF EARTH IS TO BE OUR NEW HOME, WE MUST FORGE A NEW NATION!
WE MUST COMBINE OUR STRENGTHS...
AND DEMAND THE HOME WE ARE ENTITLED TO.
STANDING ALL TOGETHER, WE LEAVE THE HUMANS WITH NO CHOICE...
THEY WILL GIVE US A HOME, OR WE WILL TAKE ONE FROM THEM!
A NEW HOME - TOGETHER!
KLANK KLANK
HE SHOULD TOTALLY BE LEADER.
KLANK KLAN
WHAT?

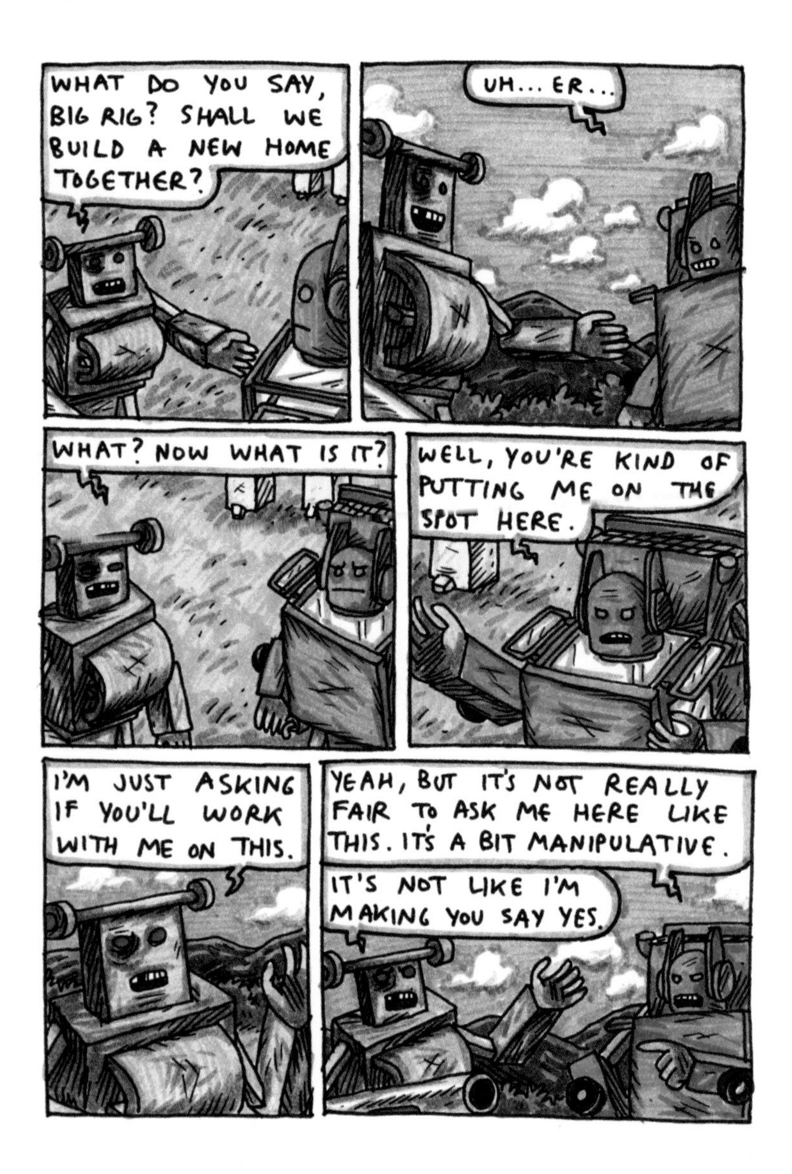
WHAT DO YOU SAY, BIG RIG? SHALL WE BUILD A NEW HOME TOGETHER?
UH... ER...
WHAT? NOW WHAT IS IT?
WELL, YOU'RE KIND OF PUTTING ME ON THE SPOT HERE.
I'M JUST ASKING IF YOU'LL WORK WITH ME ON THIS.
YEAH, BUT IT'S NOT REALLY FAIR TO ASK ME HERE LIKE THIS. IT'S A BIT MANIPULATIVE.
IT'S NOT LIKE I'M MAKING YOU SAY YES.

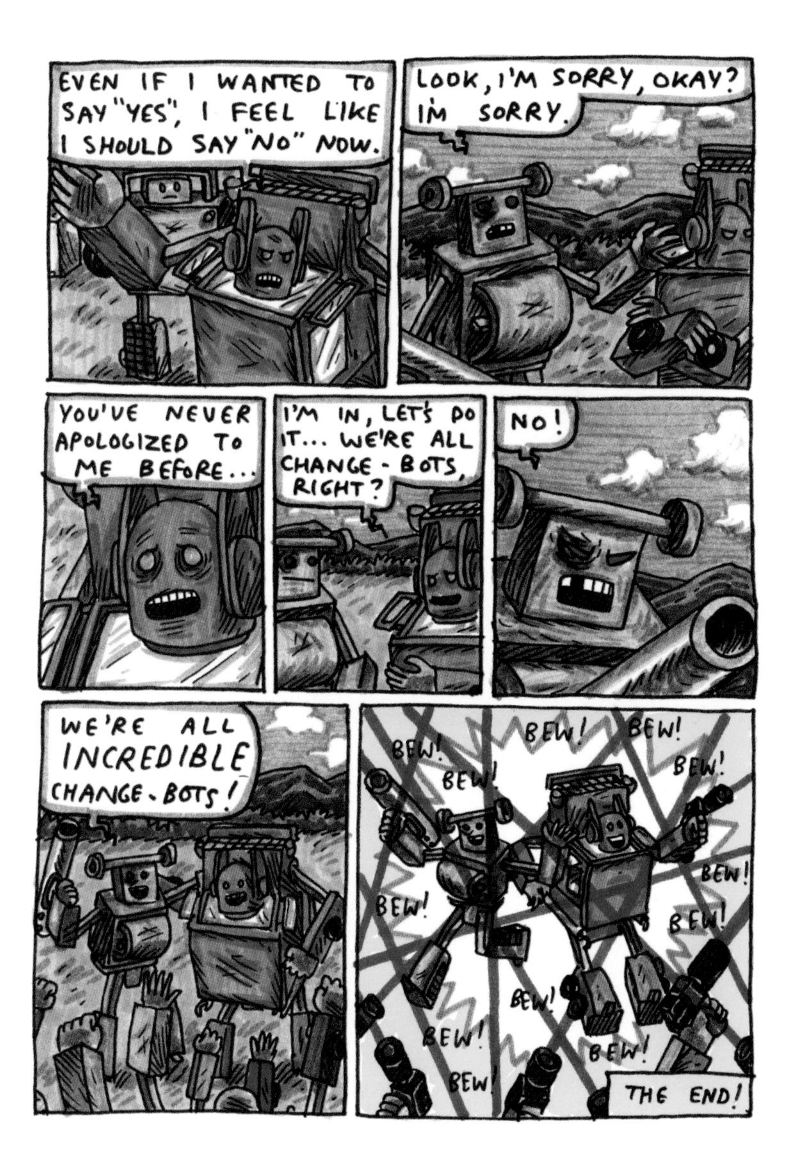
EVEN IF I WANTED TO SAY "YES", I FEEL LIKE I SHOULD SAY "NO" NOW.
LOOK, I'M SORRY, OKAY? I'M SORRY.
YOU'VE NEVER APOLOGIZED TO ME BEFORE...
I'M IN, LET'S DO IT... WE'RE ALL CHANGE-BOTS, RIGHT?
NO!
WE'RE ALL INCREDIBLE CHANGE-BOTS!
BEW! BEW! BEW! BEW! BEW! BEW! BEW! BEW! BEW! BEW! BEW! BEW!
THE END!

EPILOGUE

A FEW WEEKS LATER
SO. THIS IS PRETTY GREAT, HUH? A NEW HOME...
YEAH. GREAT.
UH...WAS THAT SARCASM?
UH, NO. IT'S GREAT. IT'S REALLY GREAT.
REALLY, REALLY GREAT.
I'M GOING TO GO TO THE TOWN HALL MEETING...
THAT'S GREAT.

OKAY, OUR FIRST ORDER OF BUSINESS IS DECIDING WHETHER AWESOMEBOTS OR FANTASTICONS GET TO LIVE IN THE SLIGHTLY LARGER EAST WING OF THE NEW FANTASTICAWESOME COMPLEX
DIBS!
YOU CAN'T CALL "DIBS."
JUST DID.
LOOK, YOU--
DIBS!
DIBS!
OKAY, FINE.
THIS IS MY MOMENT!

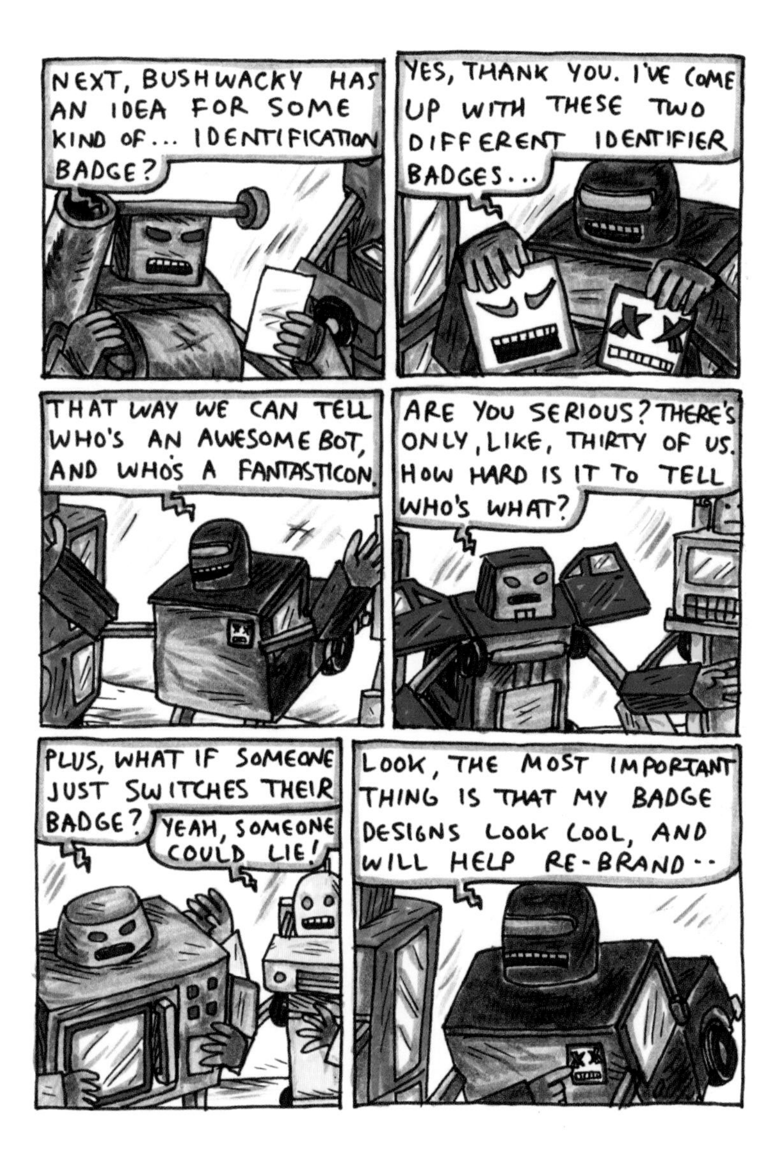
NEXT, BUSHWACKY HAS AN IDEA FOR SOME KIND OF... IDENTIFICATION BADGE?
YES, THANK YOU. I'VE COME UP WITH THESE TWO DIFFERENT IDENTIFIER BADGES...
THAT WAY WE CAN TELL WHO'S AN AWESOME BOT, AND WHO'S A FANTASTICON.
ARE YOU SERIOUS? THERE'S ONLY, LIKE, THIRTY OF US. HOW HARD IS IT TO TELL WHO'S WHAT?
PLUS, WHAT IF SOMEONE JUST SWITCHES THEIR BADGE?
YEAH, SOMEONE COULD LIE!
LOOK, THE MOST IMPORTANT THING IS THAT MY BADGE DESIGNS LOOK COOL, AND WILL HELP RE-BRAND..

RAZOW!
WHAT? YOU KNOW YOU WERE THINKING ABOUT DOING THAT!
ARE YOU OKAY, BUSHWACKY?
OHHHHH
IS IT MY... FAULT?
OKAY, MY BAD, OKAY? I WON'T DO IT AGAIN.
GEEZ.

AND THAT'S ALL WE HAVE.
THAT'S IT?
SO.
SOOOOOOO...
NOW WHAT?
SIGH.
PROBABLY TO BE CONTINUED...!

ABOUT THE AUTHOR

JEFFREYBROWNRQ@HOTMAIL.COM

P.O. BOX 120
DEERFIELD IL
60015 - 0120
USA

RECEIVE A LETTERPRESS MEMBERSHIP CARD AND COPY OF FAN CLUB NEWSLETTER FEATURING INSIDERY INFORMATION AND OTHER INTERESTING READING, ALL FOR JUST FIVE DOLLARS! (U.S. DOLLARS; INTERNATIONAL ORDERS FOR SIX DOLLARS U.S.) SEND CHECK OR MONEY ORDER TO: JEFFREY BROWN, P.O. BOX 120, DEERFIELD IL 60015-0120 U.S.A.

EMAIL CHANGEBOTS@GMAIL.COM WITH ANY QUESTIONS OR CONCERNS. PLEASE BE SURE TO INCLUDE THE FOLLOWING DATA:

NAME:
MAILING ADDRESS:

EMAIL:
MEMBERSHIP NAME:
FAVORITE CHANGE-BOT:
ANY CHANGE-BOTS RELATED QUESTION YOU MAY HAVE:

OFFER EXPIRES DECEMBER 31, 2011.
PLEASE ALLOW 4-6 WEEKS FOR DELIVERY.

THIS BOOK ISN'T "MANGA," SO YOU'LL NEED TO START READING FROM THE OTHER SIDE. IF YOU ALREADY DID THAT, YOU CAN STOP BECAUSE THE BOOK IS OVER. IF YOU'D LIKE TO KEEP READING, YOU'LL NEED TO FIND ANOTHER BOOK! HERE'S WHERE TO LOOK:

www.topshelfcomix.com/jeffreybrown

www.jeffreybrowncomics.com